I0720318

REBEL WITHOUT A CLUE

Planet Hy Man Book One

By
Kerrie A Noor

MEET THE GANG

Legless: a man from Planet Hy Man who is past his prime. No one knows why he is called Legless, but he is a man elusive as a shadow, as well as the reason for the whole saga that you are about to read.

Beryl: a woman way past her prime. She is the leader of Planet Hy Man and has been since this whole saga began—and intends to remain so.

Mex: a woman from Planet Hy Man who is angry as she is courageous. She is of the age where a pension is within her grasp and smart enough to be planning for it.

Woody: a dwarf from Earth, unemployed but young enough to still have hope.

Vegas: a young ambitious woman from Planet Hy Man. She believes in many things but is logical enough to know when to ditch said beliefs.

Hilda: a woman from Planet Hy Man who has more ambition in her little finger than an American running for president. She is in her prime and will step on anyone who dares argue.

Pete: Mex's robot—or android, as he likes to call it. Pete has plans and is smart enough to keep them well hidden.

Don: a cabbie from Glasgow with a soft spot for the character below . . .

Bunnie: a round woman who puts one in mind of Dawn French. She has a way with men, dogs, and lonely women. Except in times of stress, when she throws such "ways" to the wind for a more dominating/shouting approach.

DJ: a young DJ born in Glasgow. He is the same age as Woody and as tall as Woody is short. He is a man frustrated with his mentor, who is also the character below . . .

Archie: an Earthly pensioner who is old enough to know better and old enough not to care. His advice is ignored by many.

DBO: a teenager from Planet Hy Man. She is ignored by many, and she would like to change the status quo but is not sure how.

H2: a twenty-year-old woman from Planet Hy Man. She looks and acts much older than her years, which is probably the reason no one hangs around her.

PLANET HY MAN-GLOSSARY

Voted Ins: Planet Hy Man's politicians. A contradiction in terms as they were never voted in. In the past, they were also known as the "Blue-Rinse Brigade," when they were young enough for hair dye to make a difference.

Whip: also known as a flesh-cracker. In the past used by Man Spies to round up men like cattle during the great coup 1958, now worn like a peacock parading its virility.

Man Spy: women bred to act like men, who captured any free men to be "cared for" and/or "appropriately employed" for the greater benefit of the planet.

Manifesto the Great: the last man to rule Planet Hy Man, he wrote his memoirs while still ruling. In fact, he was so busy writing that he didn't notice the great coup of 1958 until it was too late. His last few years were spent in exile, editing the *Hy Man's Geographic*, a magazine no one had read for years, which is now mainly used for lighting fires when the price of energy goes up. It was also he who developed the early stances of the *incognito pose*.

Incognito Pose: a pose adopted by robots and the masses, helping them to blend into the background, or at least let those of great importance know that they are not worth noticing.

Teflon: a by-product of egg popping, and a material like no other. It is so flexible that a robot made of it will never age and finds yoga as easy as the mere blink of an eye.

Telespray/Telespraying: inspired by Planet Hy Man's first truly scientific woman who had a crush on *Star Trek*'s Captain Kirk. She was an enthusiastic shower-maker who designed a power shower so strong it moved women from inside the shower to outside—she saw the potential.

For a while it was all the rage for the Voted In as they telesprayed from one shop to the next, frightening shop assistants until the shop assistants rebelled and started charging *startle* charges.

Cheese Pizza: a secret passion for many on Planet Hy Man. Once someone discovered how to make hemp pulp *sort of* taste like cheese, the pizza was revived, celebrated, and eaten whenever possible. Hemp pulp never, however, managed to work in cheese sauce.

Caffeine Blast: coffee on Planet Hy Man is for the elite and was introduced mainly to keep the Voted In awake during meetings.

Illegal Beverage: caffeine for the masses is as illegal as bootlegging was on Earth. Keeping the masses alert is greatly discouraged by those in charge; weak decaffeinated tea is all they are allowed.

Egg Popping: a recently accepted profession established by the first retired man spy. Eggs (also known as valuable real-estate) from a successful woman can earn her a tidy commission—which Mex was banking on to provide her with a better robot than the damnable Pete.

Contemplation of the Navel: a practice recognized by the robot-training board as an adequate way of make the passing of time productive, as well as cutting down on minding others' business.

Arts and Stuff: anything gift-wrapped.

Limo Drivers: the last driver retired years ago and now mans the footman's residents' reception. He never remembers any names but he does a good toasted hemp pulp.

The Scent of an Identity: women who have a "longing" or a "something is missing" feeling are more susceptible to the scent than contented women. Men are completely immune.

ESP-ing: the ability to communicate without speaking aloud; a form of mind reading. Outlawed on Planet Hy Man as it made bugging —a truly profitable pastime—pointless.

Messenger: an envelope-like device that usually contained orders of an unpopular nature.

H-Pad: looks like an iPad but has the ability to answer back and is not nearly as much fun.

Sparkly: sparkling water that tastes like champagne, costs a bomb, and can cause great clarity of thought or at least the illusion of it.

Strengtheners: like straighteners, but also work as a bugging device. For years, much was collected from what women said while straightening their hair, until it was discovered that what they talked about while grooming was pretty much the said grooming. Scientists are currently working on a handless set.

CONTENT

THE LEGEND

"One day, Legless was a legend that everyone talked about, and now, years later, no one can quite remember why."
—a footman unknown and under the influence of a decent set of shoes

PROLOGUE-THE STORY

1958

On a hot afternoon, while huddled behind a hedge, Legless caught a glimpse of a woman in an apron and fluffy slippers. She was bent over her basket of washing. Legless stared at her small behind pressing against her nylon skirt and lust filled his loins. Surprised, he decided to take action—an action that had not been spoken of for many years on his planet—and soon he had the woman's rollers rattling beneath her scarf for at least two minutes.

Then he slipped away.

The woman stood up; she had felt something peculiar, but nothing too drastic. Nothing a little Epsom salts and a hair dryer wouldn't cure.

Nine months later, an Identity was born.

That year, the sales of Epsom salts soared as women all over the world, bending over their washing, had their rollers rattled like a martini: shaken but not stirred . . .

❋

Of course, Beryl was watching; she watched everything. She had installed the latest mirror for just such a purpose, and it was money well spent. Beryl took a sip of her illegal beverage and smiled. Legless was the last man on Planet Hy Man to show any sign of gumption; now she had "done away with him."

Well done, Your Sirness; well done, you!

Beryl knew Legless couldn't resist Earth—it was so, well, earthy—and she knew that a man like Legless could not withstand the temptation of an "old-style female," especially in an apron.

She poured another sparkling water, this time with extra ice. Yes, installing a two-way mirror was the height of intelligence. Not many knew about these mirrors, not even Legless, but he was easily persuaded to take one with him. Legless liked to look at himself, and he had no idea that a mirror on Earth allowed Planet Hy Man to watch, albeit with an imperfect view. Still, peering from the side pocket of a male hell-bent on getting his leg over was better than nothing—as long as you had the sound turned down.

Beryl looked at the enormous mirror she had retrieved for just such a purpose. It filled the wall and smacked of authority. She studied her face. It was a face built for power—long, lean, and with little ability to crack a smile. In fact, the nearest she ever got to a smile was a slight lift of the left side of her lip; not an attractive look for an Earth woman, but it worked wonders on Planet Hy Man.

The left side of her lip remained still as she thought about Legless. He was gone for good, no turning back.

Who needs a double-crossing man with ideas above his cycling shorts? He should have remembered who he was and, more importantly, who she was.

She pushed her beehive hair into shape. *I would have sorted the energy problems—eventually. After all, a spark plug is but a mere few bolts . . . I was almost there.*

And that's what she told herself for the next fifty years . . .

Chapter One

THE ARRIVAL

"First impressions never last." –Manifesto the Great, Hy Man's Geographic, last edition

50 years later

At half past one on a Saturday morning, Mex arrived in Glasgow. With a small bump, she landed in a bus shelter two feet away from Woody, a dwarf, who was peeing in the corner.

Woody stopped, staggered, and, like a sheep on ice, skidded to the floor. His backpack burst open and its contents scattered onto the pavement. He stared up at the vision before him. She towered over him, a giant, Gothic gran squeezed into a leather outfit even Catwoman would think twice about wearing.

Woody was scared, curious, and confused. *Is she on the pull?* He decided to lay off his mother's antidepressants for a while, worried he was hallucinating.

Mex eyed him curiously. He was collapsed in the corner like a garbage bag, wearing a facial expression she had seen many times. She sighed and looked at the contents of his backpack spread out on the ground—a book, a pen, and a packet of Quavers. She picked up the Quavers and, after a good shake followed by a sniff, tossed the packet back on the ground and then lifted the book like it was a specimen jar to be examined.

"You read these?" she said, with no interest in the answer.

Woody gulped and silently watched as Mex slid his prized Terry Pratchett into her breast pocket and pulled out a whip from her side belt.

Oh, Jesus.

The whip cracked itself around his waist and hoisted him up.

Mary Mother of God . . .

The whip twirled him around in the air and dropped him gently onto his feet—away from the piss.

"I'll be good," promised Woody. "I'll go to church."

The whip unwound from his waist and began to hover about Woody's open fly like a rattlesnake ready to pounce.

Saint Christopher Columbus . . .

The tip of the whip hooked itself around the fly lever.

"Oh. Oh. Oooh. Arrrrrh!"

Then it zipped up his fly and, with a playful tap, led Woody from the bus shelter. Woody, confused by mixed sensations of fear and pleasure, stumbled away as Mex flicked the whip back into its holder.

Woody didn't turn back once; he didn't dare. Even when whoever she was began to yell about "latrines" and the like, he didn't turn back. Fear pushed him forward, away from what, he had no idea, but he knew he wasn't hallucinating. No matter how much dope he had had, she was real.

As Woody drew closer to home, he reduced his speed to a walk, and when he saw other people, he stopped, caught his breath, and let his heart slow to a quickstep. *Everything's the same,* he told himself, *everything is okay.*

"Hey, Woody," shouted Ahmad as Woody strode past the steamy windows of the Bangladesh Tandoori. "No pakora tonight?"

Woody didn't hear. He was two doors from home and nothing was going to stop him from getting there—not even an oversized pakora and Ahmad's famous spicy dip. His stomach was churning like a washing machine; in two minutes the battered sausage and chips he had eaten earlier would be on the pavement.

Woody stopped at the front door of his flat and stared at his *knock if you dare* door knocker. His hand strayed to his fly—it was wedged tight, welded like fingers held together with superglue, stuck so fast that he broke a nail trying to pull it open. Woody knew he would never be able to undo it again. He could waste a whole can of WD-40 on his fly and still it wouldn't budge. He sighed; he was going to have to either spend the rest of his life walking around in camouflage trousers or get the scissors out.

How was he going to explain that to his mother?

The Voted In[1] on Planet Hy Man gasped; on-screen, Woody looked even more compact. They couldn't take their eyes off him; it had been a long time since anyone on Planet Hy Man had seen a man of such caliber.

"Let's track him," said Vegas to the Voted Ins. No one argued. Watching Woody would sure make this ridiculous mission worthwhile. It might even add a bit of spice.

The Voted In are a collection of women who spend their days arguing around the extra-large table in the "room with a view"—the room at the top of the Operations building where no one but the elite and some ancient footmen are allowed.

Previously called the "Blue-Rinse Brigade," they're an assortment of women who are sixty-plus and like to think that they run things, that what they say and agree on enables Planet Hy Man to run smoothly. In truth, they do little but annoy Beryl, the leader, and clutter up any decision-making with useless arguments about cushions, pizza toppings, and how tired they are of the black tuxedo uniforms that all Voted Ins wear.

Although how that came to pass as law is anyone's guess.

After the meeting, they gathered in the refreshment area. Vegas counted a full house—always the way when a new batch of illegal brew arrived. It was like Christmas . . .

At the end of the month, coffee, strong and illegal to the masses but enjoyed by the Voted In, arrived, filling the corridors of power with an aroma that had the Voted Ins' noses twitching with excitement. From their office they would poke their noses out, sniffing like it was the first time caffeine had arrived. Sipping the illegal beverage[2] in the lush surroundings of the room with a view made the tedious job of trying to appease the likes of Beryl worth it.

"This Woody," said Vegas, pouring herself a second brew. "It is agreed he is worth the watching?"

"Oh, absolutely," said one. "If we are going to have to watch reruns of this crazy mission, then Woody will make it bearable."

"Oh, and more," said another. "I mean, he has potential, don't you think?"

Vegas whisked her dairy-free milk, wondering what potential they were talking about while the others chuckled around her.

A footman coughed as he stood at the doorway—he was an elderly man dressed in a footman's uniform that hadn't changed since the post began. It was tight and shiny; in fact, it was so tight that bending to tie a shoelace was done in private, just in case any ripping occurred. It was designed when watching BBC period dramas was all the rage to match the opulent room with a view—a room with an excessive amount of chandeliers and decor that made the Brighton Pavilion look like a bog-standard B&B. All had agreed that a footman poised for action like a poor man's Napoleon Bonaparte would complement the décor.

Of course, everyone forgot that he would age, forgot that the last generation of men, made useless by technology, would shrivel like a balloon in the back of a car once their talents for procreating, story-telling, and wrestling were no longer "required."

The footman coughed again as he began to clear the table.

"Ma'am," he said to Vegas, "is it not time for your foot rub?"

----

1. *Planet Hy Man's politicians. A contradiction in terms as they were never voted in. In the past,*

they were also known as the "Blue-Rinse Brigade," when they were young enough for hair dye to make a difference.

2. *Caffeine for the masses is as illegal as bootlegging was on Earth. Keeping the masses alert is greatly discouraged by those in charge; weak decaffeinated tea is all they are allowed.*

Chapter Two

THE MISSION

"Orders are orders except when served by a footman." —an ex-footman

The Voted In, as instructed by Beryl, had issued Mex her orders. A week before Mex was sent to Earth, a meeting was held . . . while Mex was blissfully watching Pete water her patio hedge, Beryl was instigating plans.

Beryl marched into the room with a view and barked *off* to the screen, which was playing a sitcom extra loud in accents unknown and with words as unfathomable as "cannae," "ween," and "minging." Deciphering British lingo was a fulfilling pastime for many—discovering that a brolley was not actually a trolley misspelled had been one of the highlights of the week.

The screen continued to play.

"Off. Now," snapped Beryl.

The screen crackled a *ma'am* and slid back into a slit in the ceiling. The Voted In sighed. Watching reruns was the best part of their job; so far they had trolled most of the BBC and had moved on to other, lesser channels in search of a programme to keep the masses happy. They watched the programmes to reassure themselves that getting rid of men was the best thing ever, and that the threat of Earth invading them was as laughable as a footman trying to run and as believable as Beryl's insistence that her beehive hairstyle actually came from real hair. So far they had plugged away through a variety of sci-fi series, *Star Trek* being one of the favorites, as Captain Kirk was a brilliant example of how men being in control were anything but in control. And sitcoms—*Men Behaving Badly* being another favorite. It explained the complexities of a man far better than any schooling could.

"Start with the usual," said Beryl.

What?

"A messenger[1] to Mex—pronto."

Mex. The mood in the room shifted.

Beryl talked about the need for security, efficiency, and perhaps spending more than their usual budget.

The Voted In muttered quietly.

Haven't we done enough for our planet?

Mex on Earth—the cost?

Does this mean less coffee?

More spiced tea?

Beryl talked about the threat Identities posed: "They are onto us," she said, "and soon they'll be building spaceships, making contact." She looked around the room; no one met her gaze. "And it's your duty to put an end to such a threat."

Beryl continued reminding all about how the Identities could mind read—ESP—*like a pro*, calling it a "rare talent that could lead to many things," which many thought was a poor argument, as Beryl neglected to explain exactly what *many things* could be.

The Voted Ins continued to mutter.

Beryl, exasperated by the lack of enthusiasm, put on her sermon voice, her voice used to impress the masses. She pulled herself up to her full five-foot-and-three-quarter-inch height and began. The trick was to slowly increase the volume with an impressive turn of phrase.

"It is of the utmost importance that the issues on Earth—a planet as useful as an egg in a shoe—must be addressed." She looked about with her best menacing stare and increased her volume. "And suppressed! God knows what that smog-infested planet hypnotized by Sky Sports could do."

"We must be in great peril," muttered a voice from the back.

A few snickered.

"Yes," said Beryl while implementing her one-to-one glare. "Times are hard."

The women shifted about in their chairs uncomfortably; they didn't take to being stared at. A few coughed, but no one argued. Instead they stared at their beloved room with a view. They had plans for more coordination; they had set aside a budget. Now they had to cut back, thanks to some ridiculous Beryl whim about Identities *getting curious* and discovering the existence of Planet Hy Man? Many muttered under their breath. For years the Voted In had been watching the antics of the Identities and had seen nothing to suggest they were a threat—and now suddenly a mission, warranting a messenger?

Beryl looked at the clock on the wall above a footman's head, its gold-plated Georgian frame exaggerating the tired appearance of the elderly man. But Beryl didn't notice any of that; in fact, no one did. The only thing the women noticed was the time and how long it would be before Beryl's sermon finished. Beryl watched the elaborate second hand as it ticked away. Twenty minutes, that's all it took to plant a seed —*Well done, now exit and leave them shuffling*—and as the door closed behind her with an expensive swish, the women looked at each other, confused and speechless.

Legless had left more offspring on Earth than a turtle lays eggs on a beach, and up till now his offspring were considered as harmless as the said turtle eggs. Earth was full of them, and as the Voted In had watched them grow and breed, they had laughingly called them the Identities—because on Earth they had to frequently make up an identity to avoid any unwanted attention.

"All they do is meet up," said one Voted In.

"Hardly a threat," muttered another.

"They just ESP each other . . ." said a voice from the back.

"Absolutely."

"So true."

" . . . about women," continued the voice from the back, "who they have met and who they will meet, and what they are going to do when they do meet."

"Meetings."

"Exactly."

"The situation hardly calls for a messenger."

"That's no reason for us to fork out for a H-Pad [2] . . ."

"Just to satisfy Beryl's need for leadership and her fantasies."

Vegas tried to calm things down, suggesting that maybe Hilda could "sort things out."

The room fell silent, as it always did when everyone agreed. Messengers were rarely used because they always led to the use of an H-Pad, and an H-Pad cost at least a month's worth of caffeine. The H-Pad was inspired by Earth's iPad, the only difference being that shouting at an H-Pad worked as well as any keypad. Women on Planet Hy Man loved shouting at things.

The group began to grumble until the voice from the back pointed out that the mission involved getting rid of Mex: "she that makes a drama out of the past, who won't let it lie. We won't have to listen to her and that fraternity droning on about how much they saved the planet."

A few of the Voted In chuckled.

"Isn't that a bonus?"

Again, silence fell over the room as one woman looked to another until the voice from the back spoke up again. "Of course, once Hilda hears, who knows what will happen."

❋

When Beryl left the room with a view, she decided to wait. She stood at the reception desk and asked the footman for a glass of sparkly[3], and when he turned to the cooler, she slipped into the stationary cupboard by the desk. Which, with its back to the room with a view, enabled her to not only hear every word but take down notes as well.

With her ear to the wall, she listened, and as they talked of Hilda—she cursed; she had forgotten about her, the proverbial fly in the cream—Beryl pulled her portable calendar from her pocket with a jolt and hit her head against the wall. She breathed another curse and then counted the days; hopefully her timing had saved her. Bossing the

Voted In into accepting her mission was doable, but Hilda . . . it would be as easy as watering a garden in a hurricane.

The next morning, Mex had been abruptly woken in the morning by insistent knocking on her door. She had opened the door to find a knackered-looking footman leaning against the wall and panting. He was oblivious to the "Out of Office" sign on her door; running with glasses was not practical. In fact, running in the getup footmen were forced to wear was about as practical as wearing thermals to the gym. The only good thing about a runner's assignment was the sheer bliss of a cupcake once finished, with no fear of a tight waistband.

The footman pulled a lace handkerchief from his breast pocket and attempted to wipe the sweat from his brow. Mex, taking pity on her floor, handed him a wet wipe (left by the door by Pete for just such an occasion). The footman finally got his breath back and reverently accepted a glass of chilled water. And then, with the walk of someone whose shoes had no respect for his bunions, he headed back to headquarters.

Mex mulled over the footman's "this is top secret and there's more in it for you" speech and then headed back into her upwardly mobile pad. She turned the messenger she'd been given over in her hand; it was not a good sign. Messengers were a prelude to more messengers and finally an H-Pad. And an H-Pad meant a mission of travel, interception, and excessive video contact with Beryl . . .

She held out the messenger to Pete, who stared at the envelope, which looked misleadingly easy to open.

"Tell me your thoughts," she said.

Pete was in the middle of quietly pruning the hedge on the balcony. He placed his hedging implement back in its holder and took the messenger from Mex, or Her Leathership, as he liked to call her.

A messenger wasn't the easiest of things to open. *Messenger* was a posh word for an envelope so securely fastened with Beryl's "proceed at your own peril" seal that many wouldn't open at all. And it required long fingernails, not something a 33 Robot had, but Pete fumbled with elegance until Mex couldn't take any more. She flicked open the messenger and the blank paper slid out into the air while unfolding. They waited for the words to appear.

Pete read the list of orders as they appeared on the paper. "Intercept the Identities and propose—sorry, dispose." Pete looked up at his mistress. "Then come back here, ma'am, where a promotion and that nice hedge-less villa on the coast await."

Mex pulled the list from her assistant. "It's more complicated than that. Look, your mission is top secret . . ."

"My lips, ma'am, are sealed," said Pete.

"You need to establish control over the Identities; they must be kept in the dark at all costs."

"Dark, ma'am?"

Mex stared at the instructions. Beryl was always talking about darkness, "keeping a lid on things" and how "one must be frugal with the truth," and this time Mex was confused. Was Beryl being frugal with her?

Knowledge of Identities on Planet Hy Man was sparse, mainly because no one was interested. Identities were seen as large, ugly, way too full of themselves to be worth talking about, and way too stupid to worry about. However, Beryl had begun to talk to Mex of a hoard of invading Identities running amok and "stripping our energy dry," and Mex up till now had ignored her. She just assumed Beryl's rants were an age thing. She had no faith in Beryl's logic; she, like everyone else on Planet Hy Man, believed in the "men think with their appendages" theory, and the idea of Identities invading Planet Hy Man was as laughable as Beryl's hairdo.

"I'm not comfortable with this," she finally muttered. "There is more to this mission than keeping things in the dark."

Pete let out another sigh. "I tell you, a piece of cupcake."

"Cake? Cake? They are sending me down to Earth; the only thing decent about that place is the food."

"Breakfasts to die for, ma'am."

Mex looked at Pete. He had obviously been taking instruction from Beryl. And when he started to talk about Beryl's "good taste," Mex knew he had been coached. Beryl, like all women with a fondness for wearing black, had no taste, just a distaste for laundry bills.

"But look what happened to Legless—he went down and never returned. He died lost, alone, and shriveled like a pickled walnut."

"Ma'am, he is but a male, mere testicles on legs . . ."

"A pair of testicles which are now pushing up daisies; I don't want to be the next *Story* told."

" . . . whereas you, ma'am, are as hormonal as a dried tomato."

"Thanks, Pete, that's a big help," said Mex as she thrust the list into his face. "And there is no mention of a villa, you made that up."

"It's a given, ma'am," said Pete. He sniffed, then walked inside as she followed, waving the messenger in the air, a habit Pete found irritating at the best of times.

"I'm not ready for this, Pete!" said Mex. "I am a man spy, not a reporter of foreign affairs. What do I know of the ways of Earth, let alone men? I just wrap them and pack them."

"Ma'am, wrapping and packing men is a mere turn of phrase that went out with two-way mirrors and"—he sighed—"a man spy is but a distant memory from the past."

"I mean, I was born to lead, here, on this planet," said Mex. "Not explore over there."

Mex tossed the messenger into the air in disgust and with a *poof* it burst into confetti, fluttered to the ground, and disintegrated, leaving not a trace on Mex's shag pile. Here she was, the greatest man spy Planet Hy Man had ever seen, being asked—told—to go to Earth. A woman who, when she was barely out of braces, no more than a teenager, had risen to the challenge of hunting down every man in hiding and bringing them to their rightful place.

"I am a hero," she said. "I saved this planet for what—to be sent on a find-out-and-report mission?"

She watched Pete pull out one of Mex's leather suits and a tub of Betty's Best oil for leather and began to rub with vigor—like he was sanding a floor.

"I am more than a story from the past," she muttered.

Pete's usual reverence for polishing seemed to evaporate with each stroke. He was rubbing the leather like there was no tomorrow.

Normally Pete took time with his waxing—oozing the thick layers across whatever he could find, occasionally stopping to admire the shine like a craftsman. Not today. He was grunting like a hog in a trough, and Mex had a pretty good idea why. It was the same every year . . . and every year she had to make some sort of cringeworthy apology.

Well, not this year; this year she was heading for testosterone-pumped Earth and he could stuff his apology . . .

"Pete," she finally said. "Have you taken your lubrication today?"

Pete remained silent.

She sighed. "It's just that with this Earth mission I haven't got time for your . . . what do you call it again?"

Pete stopped and looked at his mistress. "Anniversary, ma'am, and may I add that lubrications are for the production robots on production lines. As I have said before, oils for someone of my caliber are as necessary as it would seem anniversary cards are to yourself."

Mex watched as Pete continued with his robust rubbing. She needed her leather intact for the mission.

"Look, I know a card is customary, but I have a lot on my mind."

Pete continued to rub.

She sighed. "Must we go through this again? It is just a card!"

"Absolutely right, ma'am. Three years of service; nothing to write home about."

---

1. *An envelope-like device that usually contained orders of an unpopular nature.*
2. *Looks like an iPad but has the ability to answer back and is not nearly as much fun.*
3. Sparkling water that tastes like champagne, costs a bomb, and can cause great clarity of thought or at least the illusion of it.

Chapter Three

PETE

"The power of Teflon has been greatly overrated." —Mex

Pete sat on his yoga mat and tried to contemplate his navel. Her Leathership would be indisposed for . . . how long, he had no idea, just as he had no idea what would happen to him. As a robot he had no choice, he just followed orders.

He knew he couldn't stay in Mex's penthouse deadheading the patio plants. And as for canceling her appointments, how long would that take him—a morning? She had written in three talks about "the great days of men rustling" for the WRI, Women's Revenue from Income Tax, and two weeks of visits to the food-hygiene plants investigating the illegal dairy trade. Some footmen still remembered the getting-milk-from-animals process and, according to Mex, some women still had a taste for it.

Also according to Mex, bribing a footman was "as easy as shouting at an H-Pad."

"They have nothing," she said. "They don't even own their own uniforms."

She was relaxing on the patio after one of Pete's famous vegan ratatouilles at the time, talking about how every morning the footmen scrambled for a uniform "like the Voted In at the coffee maker. I mean, with just the mere promise of a hot water bottle they would give away any secret, yogurt, custard, even cheese [1]sauce." Pete watched Mex's face glaze over as it always did with the mention of cheese.

"Ma'am?" Pete muttered.

"Yes, Pete, keeping a planet vegan is a lot easier on paper than in reality and pretty boring to instill, I can tell you."

"You still have your cauliflower, ma'am."

"But without the cheese, Pete, what is a cauliflower? It's like a man spy without her whip[2]—it's just not the same."

Pete rolled up his yoga mat and slotted it back into its shelf. He liked looking after the penthouse. It was high above the smells of the city and streamlined as befitting a woman of Mex's stature. It had all the modern cons that made his life easy—apart from the hedge cutter; telling that thing what to do was like trying to remind Mex of their anniversary. He had put in a request for the latest sculpting equipment, but Mex didn't have an artistic bone in her body, and she didn't even look at it; his vision of beauty, like his loyalty, was completely wasted on the likes of her.

He sighed. Where would they send him? After all, he was an experiment, a new breed of robot made from Teflon, giving him the ability to adapt, think, and create pretty things. A good idea at the time, thought many, until the Teflon-ic robots started to suggest things. In the end they were nicknamed 33s because it took at least thirty-three times to tell them to shut up before they did. Beryl put up with Pete for a week, then convinced Mex that her life would not be complete without such a companion. "He's so artistic it's laughable," she said. Mex knew her choices were limited to *yes*, *okay*, and *what a great idea*. Pete and Mex had rubbed along ever since.

There were only four Teflon-ic robots made. After annoying the Voted In with their suggestion of better ways to make coffee, coordinate and budget the running of things, the other three disappeared with a "post more suitable for their creative nature" excuse. No more were made.

What would they do with him? Was the lack of an anniversary card a sign?

Pete polished the kitchen bench, watching and waiting for herself to retire to bed. He watched her try to contact others with no success.

Mex was looking for a way out and no one seemed to be available to help. Finally, after a decent amount of coffee, she left.

"I'm off," she said, "to see Her Leadership; convince her what a terrible waste of funds this mission is."

Pete stared out of the patio into the night. He tried to see the lights of the limo but it was impossible from that height. He strained his eyes until he convinced himself that she must have left, switched on the lift alert, and pulled out her log.

Maybe there's a clue?

He flicked through the entries—three years ago . . . two years ago . . . one year . . . one month . . . finally . . .

It has been noted that the footmen's inflexibility has become a problem and Pete could be used to increase this flexibility. His yoga for robots has not gone unnoticed and perhaps could be employed to enable the footmen to be more . . . agile, to help cope with bending and things.

Pete smiled. *Not too bad an assignment.* It meant a move to quarters unknown, but he could deal with that, take a few possessions, perhaps even Mex's coffee maker.

Pete started to plan. What did he need—lubricant, mats, water bottles? He slipped Mex's log back exactly as he found it, rolled out his bed onto the patio, and stared at the Milky Way. This may be the last time he would contemplate such a spectacle, but at least he had a place, a purpose. He was not for the big Teflon-ic meltdown just yet, and of course he had his collection of logs—his insurance policy.

Beryl's back began to ache from squatting in a cupboard full of pads, pens, and staplers. She waited until the room with a view had emptied, then peeked out of the cupboard. There was no one but a footman quietly dozing. She edged the door open, skidded on some plastic wrapping, hit her head on the door yet again, and, stifling a "bollocks and bugger," crept out. Her head was now thumping in tune with the throb in her back and she decided to head for the spa; it was the only place she could be alone to think and, with the help of a footman, remove unwanted staples from unwanted places—in private—along with making adjustments to her hairdo.

Beryl slid in the back way, slung her tuxedo onto the VIP seat, and headed into the steam bath, wrapped in a towel pulverised from hemp, which the spa insisted on using. It scratched at her neck.

Bollocks and pickled egg.

She had thought that Hilda was away sorting out the "refusal to harvest at night" rebellion. She thought she could slip the mission through the system before Hilda was back. But one of the Voted Ins had talked, and now Hilda, it seemed, was not at all pleased about the whole so-called Identities crisis. Beryl thrust her towel to the wind and edged herself into the bath—mindful of her beehive.

Bollocks, pickled egg, and beetroot.

"Feet, ma'am?" said a footman poised at the end of the bath.

"Not now," muttered Beryl. "But could you survey my neck? I suspect there is something there that shouldn't be."

The footman, after a few flicks with a gloved hand, removed a splinter and went for a quiet doze on his feet while Beryl began to ponder her situation. To say that the Voted In lacked enthusiasm was an understatement, even with her latest speech and timely exit. Was she losing her grip? She reached for the glass as it plopped from the dispenser.

"Ice, ma'am?" said the dispenser.

"No."

"Ice, ma'am?"

"No . . ."

"Ice?"

"Oh for pickle's sake, no—I mean yes . . . I mean *now*."

The glass filled with sparkling water as two ice cubes clinked on top. Beryl thought about her timing, the latest energy consumption, and her options, and she was in the middle of reminding herself of the said options when a plump square hand stretched out from the bubbles like the fin of a shark and grabbed the glass before Beryl had the chance.

Beryl sighed. She knew who it was; she would recognize that shovel of a hand anywhere. It belonged to a woman who after a binge on James Bond films had never been quite the same.

"You can keep it, Hilda," she said. "I am not thirsty anyway."

Hilda's head emerged from the water, glistening and smooth like a seal until her short hair spiked up like a jackknife, giving her a more kookaburra look. "Just as well," said Hilda.

"Why?"

"Because the cost of this mission is high." Hilda drained her glass and with an *aargh* slammed it back onto the dispenser with a "no ice" command.

Beryl sighed.

"Vegas has kept me in the loop," said Hilda. With a glance at the empty glass, she snapped "now" and the glass began to bubble with water, finishing with the *plop* of a lemon slice. Hilda made herself comfortable. Beryl pulled her knees into her chest. Beryl watched Hilda slide the lemon between her lips and wondered how she got in past the footman but didn't have the heart to ask. Hilda gloating was not easy to bear.

"The Voted In are not happy," said Hilda, toying with her glass.

"When are they?" said Beryl.

"If you don't make cuts," said Hilda, "then this whole *thing* could blow up in the proverbial."

The footman opened his eyes and shut them again. Hilda with wet hair was not something you wanted to look at for too long.

"Who are you to tell me?" said Beryl.

"I am the Voted In. I speak for them, and they are not happy."

"As I said, when are they?"

Hilda eyed her opponent with an irritating smile. "Have you forgotten that you need their signature?"

Beryl stared at the relaxing aquarium planted into the wall. It didn't help and neither did the panpipe music; in fact, it was now irritating, almost on par with Hilda herself. "As I said, Earth is a threat of huge proportion—"

Hilda held up her hand, cutting Beryl short. "This is your budget," she said. "No mission will be signed off if the cost is higher than this figure . . ."

Beryl looked at the aquarium. Above it was a screen, which occasionally flashed headlines; fanfares trumpeted the arrival of such headlines to jolt those relaxing in the spar into some sort of panic attack—except for Beryl, who had devised the whole scheme. The new budget flashed across the scene as a fanfare of epic proportion filled the room, startling a blowfish into a frenzy of gulping and a sea horse into a mania of circling.

Beryl stared at the number; it wasn't even three figures.

"A mission on that? Impossible."

"Not if one goes secondhand," said Hilda, deepening her smile, "and thinks out of the box."

Hilda and Beryl argued back and forth like sisters over the last biscuit, Hilda punching the water with force; she talked of charging batteries and even using Earth equipment. Beryl's beehive began to flop. Hilda was taking this whole thinking-out-of-the-box thing too far. *Earth equipment—what next?* She had just spent the previous night convincing Mex, a woman on the verge of retirement, that traveling to Earth at her age was good for her future, her morale, and her hormones and was a safe bet. What was Mex going to say to the idea of using Earth's equipment?

"It's this or nothing," said Hilda. "The Voted In are no longer scared of you."

Beryl had no choice; she watched as Hilda rose from the bath white and wobbly. It had been a long time since she thought out of the box, but she was sure she could remember how, and she had an idea of where to start.

That night, after a decent dry and rub from the blow-dry chair, Beryl made her way to the basement. She walked past the *buggered equipment* shelf, the *you're having a laugh* equipment display, and the *when men ruined the planet* sections, all on show to warn anyone

—or at least those who could afford the ticket price—of past mistakes.

She entered the recycling area, scouring through shelves of old phones the size of an encyclopedia and cameras now made obsolete by the H-Pad. And the C-Pad, which preceded the H-Pad. The C-pad was designed by a frustrated industrialist who had more than a grudge against women. It was not only ugly but as difficult to open as a tin of corned beef. The same corned beef that led many to vegetarianism.

Beryl picked up a C-Pad and smiled as she remembered past heroic days of great decision-making. If Hilda thought she could get the better of her, she had another thing coming. *I've still got a few tricks up my sleeve,* Beryl thought. Then she spied what she was looking for—the very first H-Pad, unused and still with its self-destruct button intact.

It was designed like the 33 Robot with a similar "treat me with respect or I'm out of here" gene, which along with their large size had made them unpopular. As well as being too big for a handbag, they didn't take to shouting. Beryl told herself this could be a good thing.

She turned it about in her hand. It wasn't that big. In fact, in the dark and at a distance it looked almost like the later models except for the battery compartment, which, with any luck, Mex wouldn't notice until she was on Earth.

Beryl stared ahead. Mex was a stickler for the truth; convincing her that the planet was under threat from the Identities and their women had been even harder than persuading the penny-pinching Voted In. She had planned to tell Mex the truth when Mex had adjusted to Earth and retreat, let alone communication, was restricted. Mex could not keep anything from Pete, who loved to practice yoga with Hilda's robot.

Beryl dropped the H-Pad into her extra-large carrier bag, and slung it under her arm. Mex needed a sidekick, someone who had no choice but to follow orders, preferably with an understanding of out-of-date technology, and who was unmoved by the ranting of a know-it-all redundant man spy[3]. Beryl knew exactly who'd fit the bill, and he didn't cost a penny.

She smiled to herself—her first thinking-out-of-the-box moment in years. Pete on Earth was the perfect choice. He would know exactly what to do when she told Mex that Planet Hy Man's energy was on its last legs, and it was all thanks to a stupid decision the great and esteemed leader had made years ago.

---

1. *A secret passion for many on Planet Hy Man. Once someone discovered how to make hemp pulp sort of taste like cheese, the pizza was revived, celebrated, and eaten whenever possible. Hemp pulp never, however, managed to work in cheese sauce.*
2. *Also known as a flesh-cracker. In the past used by Man Spies to round up men like cattle during the great coup 1958, now worn like a peacock parading its virility.*
3. *Women bred to act like men, who captured any free men to be "cared for" and/or "appropriately employed" for the greater benefit of the planet.*

Chapter Four

THE SHED

"To find a room for one's thoughts is as important as finding room for one's shoes." —Pete's log

Back in the fifties, when Beryl was young and just another Voted In working her way up, men were the only source of energy. No longer needed for breeding, they were enslaved in gyms under the city, where they completed eight-hour shifts of spinning on stationary bikes, rowing on stationary rowing machines, or walking, for the less able, around the room.

Beryl, who everyone knew to be a no-nonsense, tell-it-like-it-is sort of woman, had been assigned to "sort out any rumblings" that may occur in the gym. So, when the "man can not cycle on bread alone" campaign took hold, Beryl was there to silence any rebellion.

Beryl marched to the basement and came across a sea of men in Lycra spinning their hearts out on stationery bikes like cyclists at a Tour de France with no sign of any rumblings . . .

"Come on, lads, keep it up, four hours to pint time," shouted Legless.

Beryl took one look at his pert butt in the air and her heart began to race. She wanted to wake up every morning to the view of his taut thighs peddling his gluteus off and, without even thinking, offered Legless a stationary with a view, glucose drinks, and Lycra that breathed.

Legless became her personal energy source. She woke every morning to his clenched buttocks working overtime for her coffee machine, her strengtheners[1], and her top-of-the-range create-your-own-log equipment. Until, that is, he and she came up with the idea of recyclable energy without a cycle.

"Alls you need are a few spark plugs," he said, and Beryl wondered why she hadn't thought of it.

Men were aging and not being replaced—new sources of energy were needed. Beryl took the idea to the Voted Ins and immediately got her promotion, her portrait in the council chambers, and the penthouse with a view. She now had the best seat at the meeting table, first read of all minutes, and the attention of everyone worth impressing. And she had every intention of sharing her success with Legless. She had plans to surprise him with a deluxe saddle on his stationary bike, along with ice for his glucose drinks and as much illegal beverage as he wanted. But Legless, *damn it*, wanted more. He wanted his name beside hers and to share her seat and privileges.

Legless—"full of himself" and angry—seduced the men into a revolt. He sucked them into a frenzy of demands until suddenly they, the men who were happy with a good back scrub and a pint at the end of the week, wanted "better conditions" and a change of uniform: "Lycra that moves, breathes, and doesn't damage the goods," shouted many.

Beryl snorted at the memory. *As if anyone was interested in the safety of out-of-date goods.*

"I helped her save the planet," Legless shouted, poised on a running machine mid shift, and wrote his own warrant of exclusion. Legless was sent to Earth.

Why did he have to want so much? thought Beryl. He had a great view right near the patio, he could spin all day, watching the sun rise and set, with a ten-geared stationary—*I mean who else had gears on their stationary? He was even allowed a break or two; after all, how much cycling does it take for a pair of strengtheners?*

Beryl thought they were close; they dreamed the same dream. *What a fool.*

But what hurt the most was the hidden betrayal.

Beryl had kept instructions for spark-plug-making in the potting shed, just in case. Years later, with Legless lost somewhere in the wilds of Scotland and the last spark plug winding down, Beryl confidently trotted to her potting shed and rummaged under her hedge seedlings only to find nothing but a "you shag me and I'll shag you" note—*so typical of Legless.*

Two months later, she still was no closer to a solution and time was running out; it all hinged on Mex and Pete, and neither had heard of a spark plug let alone how to make one. But they could find the whereabouts of Legless's hiding place for it. Of course, Beryl did have a plan B; all good leaders had a plan B even if it was just an escape plan. But she didn't want to think about that. She wanted to believe that plan A was the one and only plan and that Mex would, in the end, embrace her vision. Although *embracing things* was not Mex's strongest talent.

*H*ilda left the spa with great speed. So impatient was she to get to the next part of her plan that she rebuffed the footman's offer of a pedicure, told the blow-dry chair to shove it, and flicked the hemp towel across her back, allowing other bits to drip-dry.

Still buttoning up her suit, she dashed into the security exit, ducking the view of the cameras in the corner. The shed was her next stop . . .

She took the old servants' route, a route that many had forgotten. It involved navigating passages, crouching in a dumbwaiter, and running, still crouched, through a lean-to the height of a table. But for Hilda, a few minutes of crouching was a small price to pay for getting what she wanted.

It took her ten minutes to arrive at the shed, appearing from nowhere—a talent that made being in control that much easier.

The shed was where the masses aspired to be. It was the ultimate place to work for all those born the wrong side of the track, where free education taught you little apart from how great the Voted In were.

The shed was where the Operators collected information and,

under the instruction of Beryl, filtered it for the Voted In and, after even more filtering, allowed it out to the masses.

Hilda, however, had taken to entering on a whim. Having worked in the shed years ago, it was easy for her, and surprising the Operators was an added bonus—like ducking the security cameras.

"All hands on deck—Mex is going down and without an H-Pad," she said.

The shed, in silence, stared at Hilda. Without an H-Pad . . . what was she talking about?

"Beryl has gone to the basement," said Hilda.

A few gasped.

"It seems she's intent on some sort of recycling." Hilda laughed. "I mean, what she will find there is anyone's guess . . ."

"H-Pad, ma'am," said a voice from the back.

"What? How?" Hilda stared into the dark. "Where did she get the okay for that sort of funding?"

"Second hand."

"Second hand? I thought they were all destroyed," said Hilda.

It was explained to Hilda that destruction, recycling, and dumping were pretty much all the same thing . . . Hilda looked on in disbelief as the "you never know when you might need it" theory was explained.

"Even a footman didn't believe in that," said Hilda.

*B*eryl, unaware of Hilda's visit, decided to take the H-Pad to the shed for advice. She did think about ordering the limo but decided secrecy was the best—everyone knew limos were bugged. One of her own ideas, which now it seemed had backfired.

Beryl took the stairs down to the ground floor and headed through the kitchen, which had two footmen standing at the rear and automated arms chopping, slicing, and blending on various benches. Two elderly women oversaw everything, which involved cracking jokes, forcing the footmen to taste the new recipes, and ordering the apprentices about.

It was the kitchen of new cuisine, where plant food was manipulated into meat-like objects as convincing as Hilda's sympathetic smile.

"Where's that Lila now?" shouted the dark old lady.

The other pointed to the doorway where a sorry-looking young girl was plucking thin whispers of hairs from an herb for a stew.

"What she doing that for?" said the dark lady.

"Cheek," said the fairer one. "She'll not answer me back again."

The young girl looked up from the doorway, peering at the rows of benches blocking her view. Through the space she saw Beryl's beehive passing by and for a minute stopped, panicked, and then raced inside.

Beryl headed out the back and walked through the grounds of hedges and Zen rock designs. She made her way to the shed, ducking wind chimes about the entrance.

The wind chimes hadn't chimed since Hilda left the shed. She had cemented them together with an experimental tofu which, when cooled, had the constancy of concrete. The last thing Operators needed as far as Hilda was concerned was peace and tranquility.

Beryl waltzed into the shed, using every ounce of energy to look like she was in control. Her masked face twitched as the Operators in command stopped and stared.

"A few questions," said Beryl.

The dashboard Operators looked up. *Since when did the esteemed ask questions?*

Beryl placed the H-Pad on the dashboard and let out a nervous cough. A small bead of sweat slid from the corner of her beehive, but in the dark, no one saw. The Operators gathered about the dashboard in silence. The first in command turned the H-Pad about and poked at the battery compartment. The first in command had never seen one before.

"Hilda says that charging this is possible on Earth because the atmosphere is—how did she put it—kind?" Beryl coughed again. This time, the first Operator in command noticed.

"Hilda said this?" said the second Operator in command.

"Well, in a manner of speaking."

The first in command handed the H-Pad to the second. "Well, I guess if Hilda says . . ."

The second in command looked at the third in command. "What do you think?"

The third in command whistled through her teeth. "Yes, well, it might work, but you'd be better off with the new model—I mean, why aren't you taking that?"

"Budget," said a voice at the back.

The first in command threw her a "shut it" look.

Beryl was getting impatient; she had to get things sorted, get Mex up and running on Earth. She wanted to hear that it was okay. "Well, is it?"

The third in command took the H-Pad, turned it about, and sniffed . . .

"If Pete has his plugulator, you're laughing," said the dashboard Operator.

Beryl stared at the slip of a girl speaking to her—the last thing she was looking for was a laugh.

---

1. *Like straighteners, but also work as a bugging device. For years, much was collected from what women said while straightening their hair, until it was discovered that what they talked about while grooming was pretty much the said grooming. Scientists are currently working on a handless set.*

Chapter Five

THE SIDEKICK

"A flick with a whip is worth two kicks at least." –Man Spy Manual

The day after Mex had received her orders, more orders arrived. Pete had just finished giving the hedge-cutting implement a good "going over" with Betty's Best oil for implements when the doorbell rang. As Her Leathership was packing at the time, Pete answered the door, muttered a "thank you," and passed a few extra wet wipes to the footman as the footman handed an H-Pad to Pete.

Pete took the H-Pad inside.

"Argh, one of *those pads*," said Mex, attempting some lighthearted banter. "No expense spared, I see."

Pete ignored her.

Mex was annoyingly scratchy, and ridiculously hopeful. "Maybe it's good news," she muttered. Maybe they had changed their minds and she could, as she said to Pete, "remain here on Planet Hy Man and not face men and their midnight shadows after all!"

"Five-o'clock, ma'am."

"What?" said Mex.

"Five-o'clock shadow, ma'am, and H-Pads are usually used for transportation purposes; it's their portability that makes them so . . ." He looked at it again. "Portable?"

Mex stared at Pete. "Portable? I'll need a suitcase for that."

"So it would seem, ma'am."

"I mean, if the STD—State-of-the-Art Tech Department—can get rid of stupid plastic packaging, why can't they make an H-Pad easy to carry? Look at this," she said. "It's bigger than Beryl's beehive hair. I've seen postage stamps with a better design than that." She tossed it across her bed.

Pete sighed. Her Leathership, as usual, was making a banquet out of things.

"It'd be easier to open one of those out-of-date soya-slice packets than connect with that thing."

"H-Pads," said Pete, "have feelings too, you know, and it would be wise, ma'am, to remember what side the soya slice is sitting on. Ma'am will be partnered with said H-Pad for the duration of the mission; best to try and oil the proceedings, so to speak."

Mex, ignoring Pete, moaned so much that the H-Pad soon kicked up a fuss as predicted by Pete, such a fuss that it took all morning for them to make a connection. By the time they did, the light had gone, Mex's patience had evaporated, and Pete's new take on an old-style ratatouille was sitting in the bin, smoldering away like last night's campfire.

"*You have selected option one; this is incorrect. Please try again . . . please try again . . . please try again,*" said the H-Pad for what seemed the hundredth time.

Typical, thought Mex. *In a few hours' time I am going on a mission to a city that is famous for an accent that even the English don't understand, and I am supposed to take a wisecracking H-Pad.*

"*Please try again.*"

Mex in the end gave the H-Pad a good bash, causing so much coughing and spluttering from the H-Pad that she was about to toss it into the bin, calling her/it among other things a "drama queen."

Pete finally took over, caressing the keypad with an Android's appreciation of a fellow kind. The H-Pad purred.

"Getting a clearer picture now," said Pete as a small fanfare began to play.

"Hear ye! Hear ye!" said the H-Pad. *"Her Sirness is about to dress up the situation."*

"It's Beryl, our great and esteemed leader," said Pete.

"Her Supreme-ness is addressing—"

"Thank you, H-Pad," said Beryl as her powerful face came into view. "Evening, Mex."

"Sirness."

Beryl peered into the screen. "You've had your hair dyed."

"Kind of you to notice, ma'am."

"Takes years off you," said Beryl.

"Blonde is so aging," said Pete.

Mex glared at Pete as the screen panned out from Beryl's face, showing a backdrop of silk curtains framing a portrait of her—the esteemed leader, younger, leaner, with deep red lips and a black bouffant beehive hairstyle of the fashion decades ago.

Mex and Pete had been forced to sit on the swinging deck chair because the H-Pad refused to connect anywhere else. And it was a tight fit, even for Pete and Mex's trim frames. But as Mex had paid a fortune for it and Pete had recommended it, neither said anything. Rather, they sat like tense strangers trying not to touch—not easy on a chair that swung with the slightest movement.

"We have a situation on Earth we need to *address* . . ." Beryl said.

"So you say," muttered Mex.

"I warned the Voted In about this, but did anyone listen?"

"Do they ever, your Sirness?" said Pete.

"No, Pete, they don't; too busy getting down with their sci-fi and sitcoms—how can anyone talk about *Men Behaving Badly* when Legless's offsprings are free to roam, I ask you?"

"Men behaving badly?" said Mex.

"Yes, ma'am, a mildly funny sitcom of the nineties that many assumed is a literal guide to men behaving, err . . . badly."

"Absolutely, Pete," said Beryl.

Mex eyed her increasingly sucking-up robot; he was making her position worse and she decided to argue her case. Granted, Legless had spread his seed far and wide and there were now generations of Identities on Earth. But as no one on Earth had a clue—what was the point in trying to fix the situation?

"But, Sirness," said Mex. "They just roam about and drink coffee—what's the problem?"

"Roam; they do more than that," said Beryl. "They have half the female population hanging on their every word!"

"Half?" said Mex. "I find that hard to believe."

"And women can be a powerful force," said Beryl. "Look at us, what we have achieved. Once those Identities start to influence women, what will they do? Will they learn to read the Identities' minds, start to make spaceships, visit us, boss us about, take over even? We can't just sit still. We must scan this Earth—"

"We?" said Mex.

"Attempt some sort of control—"

"Control of what?" said Mex.

Beryl's slim lips clenched. "We must send down the best there is."

"That's you, ma'am," muttered Pete to Mex.

"And the most discreet," continued Beryl.

"Your good self again, ma'am."

"Sirness," snapped Mex, "is all this absolutely necessary? I mean, Earth is so not now!"

Beryl tutted—must she really go through all this again? Next time she'll remember to have all persons implicated in a mission attend the same meeting.

"We are talking about the Identities," continued Mex, "what is there to worry about? I mean their mothers are from Earth, it's not like they can think."

"What?" said Beryl.

"Think," snapped Mex. "Humans are not known for their thinking? They are known for their smash-and-grab, blame-it-on-someone-else philosophy. They excel at weapon-making and animal-killing. The last thing on a human's mind is thinking about new ways to fly to the moon and beyond, unless of course there was some sort of energy source they could steal."

Beryl coughed uncomfortably.

"No, humans do not plan, learn, or take thinking seriously," said Mex.

"Apart from a sitcom, ma'am, or sports, or for that matter dogs," said Pete.

"*Legless did,*" said the H-Pad with a sickening smugness.

"She has a point there."

"Shut up, Pete."

"With the Legless gene on Earth, who knows what it may lead to," continued Pete.

"I said shut it."

"Which is why we need . . ." continued Beryl.

"The best," said Pete.

"*The most up-to-the-minute technology,*" said the H-Pad.

Mex glared at the H-Pad. "You serious?"

" . . . Pete to accompany you," said Beryl.

Mex asked her to repeat it three times. *A robot on Earth—whose idea was that?*

Pete was so taken aback that he lost his balance. The swing chair reacted swiftly to the tension in his rigid buttocks and swung back too quickly for Pete and Mex to follow and they both landed on the ground.

Peter argued against the trip, picking himself up in the process, which didn't add much weight to any argument. Not that there is much a robot can do to argue apart from stuttering, "But . . . but You're Greatness." And even that was pushing it.

"The committee has stated that 'Pete's capabilities exceed his post,'" said the H-Pad. "And therefore you must accompany me and *her.*"

"I am but a mere robot, ma'am, what could I possibly do?" said Pete. "I am a coordinator, not an Operator, I am not programmed for such things, I clip hedges . . ."

"You are an Android," said Beryl, "and never forget it."

Pete tried to protest. "But my yoga classes . . ."

Beryl chose not to hear; instead she pressed the "leader is leaving" fanfare button on the H-Pad and turned up the volume. Trumpets filled the air as Beryl's face began to fade, leaving just a silhouette of her gray, extra-large beehive hair blending into the background.

Her Leadership has left the building flashed up on the screen.

Mex looked at Pete, and for the first time since talk of this ridiculous mission, Mex smiled. Watching Pete suffer pleased her to no end. "I hear the food is good down there. They batter everything, I believe."

*P*ete retired to sulk on his yoga mat. He was expected to operate an out-of-date recording system with the most opinionated man spy on the planet. Mex and her infallible ego—how many hours had he spent on the patio staring at the Milky Way while listening to how she saved the planet from men, and now he must do it all over again on Earth. Just when he thought he would get a break from it. More stories of how, when she was young, she hunted down men outlawed from any place of authority, men made obsolete by technology and no longer required for breeding, and how it was she who rounded them up and deposited them like cattle to the only place left for men: the basement.

What had he done to deserve this? The hedge-cutting implements could wait; everything could wait. In fact, Her Leathership could stuff her hedge-cutting equipment and even toss it off the balcony. He was heading for the biggest rust bucket in the galaxy—what did he care?

He opened his precious plugulator and tried to think.

*T*he plugulator is a headset worn by robots, making them accessible to their employer when indisposed. This is where Pete kept his collection of logs. One day he hoped to publish them and become the first robot to make it outside domesticity and obedience; maybe even get a little appreciation from Herself . . .

Pete first starting writing logs for his acrobatic yoga training. Pete with his Teflon-ic leather was so flexible he could, if he wanted to, bite his toenails. Not that a robot of such caliber as he would. However, Pete did hold acrobatic yoga classes for the old and infirm robots, with the use-it-or-lose-it philosophy, and for a while he became something of a guru to robots. When the Voted Ins heard about his classes, they asked him to teach their PA (Personal Android), which amused Mex no end.

She had been standing in the kitchen when Pete had told her, watching him pack her tiffin lunch box for the day. She asked him what his plans were with a casual glance at the hedge and when Pete explained about his other job, Mex was taken aback.

"They want you to go to their home and teach their robots how to bend?"

"Yes, ma'am; it appears that the new version lacks that ability."

"At their place of work?"

"Yes, PAs are discouraged from meeting with the factory/production robots. They are to be trained at home, being that they are a cut above the rest."

PAs were similar to the 33 Robot except for the elimination of the "thinking for yourself" and "ask first" genes. And removing this gene had caused a side effect of stiffness on par with a stick insect. It wasn't uncommon for a PA to do his back in fluffing a sheet, and lubrication didn't seem to help.

Mex looked at Pete as he began to roll up his yoga mats into thin columns of rubber.

"So it seems your ability to backbend while whisking a soya drink has spread the breath of our city?"

"So it seems," Pete had said, pulling another yoga mat from the cupboard.

"Flexing in a suit of minerals?"

"Ma'am, minerals are for tablets and flexing is more for your whips."

Mex wanted to know what homes Pete went to; did he teach Hilda's and Beryl's Androids?

Pete had quoted the Incognito Secrets Act that "all us Androids must abide by."

Mex had called him a robot, continuing on with the jokes about body butter oils and Vaseline.

"Ma'am, Vaseline is purely for the lubrication of spark plugs—which are these days completely out of date."

Now, Pete flicked through his logs. The first log was all about the art of lubrication . . . explaining that while "a mere inhalation of soya oil was enough for him; it was a complex process for the PA." It had taken him several nights to write this log sitting on the patio with Mex's running brook music playing in the background. Which after several trips to the toilet she turned off . . .

A PA requires thick cooking oil dripped into the ear and then plugged with a Teflon pad, after which he must circle like a dog chasing its tail for at least ten minutes. This will ensure that all joints are warmed for any yoga pose.

But soon Pete moved on to more interesting subjects to log about. He decided to expand his logs by collecting copies of other logs. While his students spent their lessons twirling or posing—eyes closed—Pete investigated and copied.

He collected from everyone—Beryl's "Manifesto to Manifesto the Great,[1]" Hilda's "Magna Carta is a Starter," and "The Vegas Diaries," which was more like a report than anything else. He copied them all—even Mex's.

At night, Mex dictated her log while reclining on the swing chair. Pete, after finishing his evening clear-up, would flop on his yoga mat, stating that he was shutting down to regenerate. After muttering a few *Ooooms* he would close his eyes in silence and wait . . .

"You present, Pete?"

"Just rebooting, ma'am."

And with the shout of an "On now," Mex would begin her latest log.

Of course, anyone who came from the Robots-R-Us area of the city would know that rebooting had gone out with cheese slices. But Mex had no idea, just as she had no idea that Pete had a photographic memory of the verbal kind. As she ranted about Beryl, Hilda, and the useless Voted Ins, Pete with a large inhale of his stomach could record. And it didn't take him long to find her past logs about the glory days of shifting men from out of their hiding places. He stored all Mex's stories onto his plugulator, from "Men, a Chromosome Short of Y" to "Beryl before the Beehive."

Pete became braver—a robot could go to places no one else knew about. He started to loiter incognito about the corridors of power under the guise of the "I have a message for Herself, is she here?" comment. The footmen never noticed, especially when slipped a small espresso.

Pete filled his plugulator with every log he had collected, and packed it. If he was going to Earth, so were his logs.

---

1. *The last man to rule Planet Hy Man, he wrote his memoirs while still ruling. In fact, he was so busy writing that he didn't notice the great coup of 1958 until it was too late. His last few years were spent in exile, editing the Hy Man's Geographic, a magazine no one had read for years, which is now mainly used for lighting fires when the price of energy goes up. It was also he who developed the early stances of the incognito pose.*

Chapter Six

THE TAXI DRIVER

"Running with dignity requires more than underwire." —Mex at the first WRI conference

At half past one on a Saturday morning, while Mex was scaring the insides out of a dwarf, Pete had been telesprayed to Dunoon. With two flashes and a "hold your breath" command from Beryl, Pete closed his eyes and opened them again to find himself standing on the top of some scaffolding staring into a sea of faces, most of whom were inebriated. This was what he was dreading; this was the reason that when he got his orders to follow Her Leathership he nearly choked on his soya oil. He had been thrust into the world of earthly pleasure and was staring into the faces of men and women who were speaking English, and he didn't understand one word.

Mex, still at the bus stop, looked at Woody's Terry Pratchett book, interested and yet confused. She had no idea that people were staring. Mex was so engrossed in Terry Pratchett *on paper*—something she had not experienced on Planet Hy Man—that three buses had driven by and reversed back; one even wound down the window and shouted "Porno Gran!"

Mex flicked the pages back and forth. She had heard about paper, but somehow, once held between the fingers, it was so—disappointing.

Finally, as instructed by Beryl, Mex headed towards the West End. "Look for a reputable B&B," Beryl had said. "I hear the breakfasts are something else." Mex had B&B information care of Beryl, a traveler's backpack meticulously packed by her assistant, Pete, and a list a mile long, which some would consider a book.

She looked down the road, ignoring the waves and horn-tooting from the cars, assuming that it was customary to shout remarks about "wanting some." Mex had foolishly believed in what she had been told. That on Earth, leather worked on all levels—and as for a whip, the larger the better, *apparently*, and if it was waving about your person like the tail of a cat, all the better!

*M*ex opened her B&B leaflet at the top of Great Western Road and started walking. The rain splashed on her leather with little effect as she stared at the houses on the side of the empty road. Bricks, and roughcast; she could not believe it, but Pete was annoyingly right. Just as he was right about the driving. They drove like there was a fire somewhere and splashing puddles on the odd walker would somehow put it out. Mex hated it when Pete was right and made a mental note not to mention the buildings, the driving, or the fact that Beryl's "open house" theory was also looking, as Pete said, "out of date."

Mex arrived at the top of Byers Road and stared at a road full of color, light, and sound. She stared at the variety of folk as they tumbled out of a Gothic-looking building with music pulsating from God knows where and in time to the lights that circled the spiral. Mex was almost impressed, until she noticed the women teetering on high heels with more flesh exposed than covered while their hair obeyed every whim of the wind. They appeared to have absolutely no aware-ness of the rain and a willingness to laugh at anything, even when they tripped and fell.

Mex wondered just how many colors one head of hair could have.

"Excuse me, my good lady," said Mex to a woman clutching onto a man like he was the mast of a sinking ship. "Your shoes," she continued, "are they not for keeping feet dry?"

The woman looked into the eyes of the leather-clad granny dressed for a fetish party for the retired—granted she was glamorous and fit, with an *I am retired but that doesn't stop me* sort of stance, but she was still a granny, old enough to remember life before a remote control—what was she thinking?

The woman stared and stumbled against her man and was just about to say something that required half a bottle of vodka to be considered witty when her man slid his arm around her shoulder, drew her lips to his, and planted a big sloppy kiss somewhere between her lips and her nose.

Mex watched, waiting for the woman to retaliate, and nearly choked on her neckband. The woman not only didn't retaliate but laughed and planted an even bigger, noisier, longer kiss straight onto his lips. Mex took appropriate action with a swift flick of her whip that was so fast no one saw; the crack echoed down the street followed by a yelp from the man.

The young man rubbed his arm while letting out a string of unrecognizable words, which Mex didn't hear. The wind had blown her B&B leaflet from her hands and she followed it down Great Western Road at a speed that had many couples staring, mid snog.

A cabbie with a fondness for athletic women in leather watched. It was an impressive sight, a woman past her prime running like an Olympic stud. He watched as she pulled her whip from her belt and stabbed the leaflet with a precision that had him dreaming of more than his usual three-in-one Saturday-night takeaway. He pulled up beside her, wound down his window, and wondered if his luck was in.

"You wanting a lift?" he said.

She looked up.

"Bunnie's?" said the cabbie without blinking an eye.

Mex went with her hunch and said yes. She jumped into the cab as the cabbie put his car into first gear. She staggered onto the seat and fumbled with her backpack, her whip, and a very wet and now useless leaflet.

The cabbie watched in his mirror, idly wondering exactly where the zip would be for such an outfit and whether he still had it in him.

"Graveyard shift, huh?" he finally said. "Not much on a Sunday morning and the rain don't help."

Graveyard? she thought, dumping her backpack on the floor. *Shifting?*

"What's your name, sweetheart?"

She looked at the cards attached to the back of the cabbie's seat. Sheila's Wheels was the first she noticed. *A good incognito name . . .*

"Aussie, huh? What you doing over here, then, Sheila? Don't the rain piss you off?"

"I have a job to do," said Mex. "Once that's done, I'll be off faster than a cat with his tail on fire!"

The cabbie stared at the road ahead. He'd never met a working girl who talked like she read books before.

He pulled up by a shabby side street. On the corner was Bunnie's Establishment. With one inhale, Mex knew her instincts were buggered; she couldn't smell anything, not one clue. All she could smell was the rain on the pavement and that was not going to help.

Mex left the cabbie with some money and just the smallest whiff of something unfamiliar yet sweet lingering in the car. The cabbie took in a deep breath and looked down at the fifty-pound note. "Your change?" he yelled. Mex dismissed him with a wave of her hand and walked down a side alley that led to the entrance to Bunnie's Establishment.

The cabbie watched the rain splatter off her leathers and then looked down at the fifty-pound note again. "The name's Don if you're ever wanting a lift," he shouted into the air, "but you can call me Donnie or Don."

Mex never heard; after all, since when did a man have something worthwhile to say? Instead she marched on until she saw Bunnie's red light glowing in the porch and knew she had found an "entrance."

Don looked down at the fifty again, crisp and new. The queen had a smirk on her face like she was sitting uncomfortably and enjoying it.

"She must be something else," he muttered before pulling out a smoke. "I never met a working woman with a fifty before."

Chapter Seven

BUNNIE'S

"An entrance is everything." —Pete's log

Mex walked into the side entrance of Bunnie's Establishment and waited for her eyes to adjust to the light. In its day, Bunnie's Establishment had been the sort of establishment where leather and whips didn't look out of place. It had been the sort of establishment that was open all night and looked shut during the day. And the sort of establishment where someone looking like Mex could have earned a lot of money.

But Mex had no idea about that sort of thing. No one did on Planet Hy Man.

Mex rang the bell and inhaled the pungent smell of sausages and Air Wick. The entrance was small, with just enough room for a couple of umbrellas, a doormat with "enter at your peril" written on it, and a small window at the side of the door with smoky glass, clean, with no view. In fact, the whole entrance was spotless.

A short, plump woman appeared from nowhere in an outfit that made getting into or out of a car almost pornographic. She had a ton of necklaces sitting on the sort of chest that got in the way of everything, including painting your toe nails. And, as she walked, the necklaces bounced on her chest like balls on a bouncy castle. A mesmerizing sight for many a man, despite her age.

In her time, Bunnie had been a catch and had earned a fortune, but thanks to a bad choice in men, Bunnie had lost most of it and was now forced to rent out her rooms and make fry-ups in the morning. Not something she was good at; in fact, the smell of bacon often brought back memories of a time she would rather forget.

She looked at Mex's slim waist and smiled to herself; that was not the sort of waist that would want a fry-up in the morning. That was the sort of figure that lived on low-fat yogurt and prunes; she was sure she had a tin somewhere.

"I would like a room, good woman," said Mex, "if you please."

Bunnie stared at Mex and wondered where she had been in such a getup. Sure, she was past her best—you could tell by the neck—but she obviously worked out. Her arms were the arms of a wrestler, muscles that stretched the leather like a way-too-small condom.

This was a woman who made Wonder Woman look like a frump. She had a square face and strong-looking hips that gave her the seductive appeal of a granny who could hold on.

Bunnie unplugged the bell, cutting short the third Bollywood tune on a harmonica, and Mex's foot stopped tapping. "Where you from?" said Bunnie. "Never seen you before."

Mex stared at the Bangladesh Tandoori carry-out menu on the wall and thought on her feet. Something she knew she was good at.

Bunnie threw her another look. "Fifty quid and I ask no questions."

"And breakfast?"

"You taking the piss?"

"Oh, piss? I never take—but I am hungry."

Bunnie pushed a key across the desk with an "aye, right" comment. "Look, Sheila from Bombay! You keep clean and I don't ask no questions!"

"And breakfast?"

Bunnie looked at Mex's expensive leather. She took in the array of tools swinging from Mex's belt, not unlike the redundant tools hanging in her own glass cabinet, and thought on her feet, something she knew she was good at.

"Breakfast is extra!" she said.

*P*ete had arrived in Dunoon to a captive audience and a round of applause.

He had arrived in the middle of a street party run by the Baptist Youth Club and the Dunoon Community Radio. But as it was an eighties retro street party most of the audience were the parents of the said Youth Club. The women were mainly dressed in some sort of Madonna guise and the men as George Michael and Spandau Ballet lookalikes, except for the DJ. He was dressed as Boy George, and he played every single Boy George song he could find.

Poof! Boom! Fizzle . . .

The smoke cleared and Pete "materialized" on the top of a scaffold in front of the Bough Hall with a jolt and a small skid.

"What the fuck!" shouted one of the few younger boys just before being slapped about the ear from an overweight Madonna spilling out of a wedding dress.

Pete attempted to regain his balance on thin wooden slats and quickly jumped into the incognito pose[1]. He stared down below at the street. It was full of unrecognizable people dancing to some sort of unrecognizable music. The beat pulsated through his Teflon[2].

The Operators had not taken into account the flexibility of a Teflon-ic robot when entering the coordinates, because it was unheard of for a robot to materialize anywhere other than on Planet Hy Man. So Pete had landed across the water from Glasgow in a place of which neither he nor anyone on Planet Hy Man had heard.

For those getting down on Boy George and the like, Pete looked like one of those gold performing "street statues" that had plagued cities during the eighties. And the fact that the plugulator looked like a head mic only increased the illusion that he was some sort of surprised performer.

Pete listened to the applause rippling through the chilly night air. Was his incognito pose not working?

He found himself forcing a smile as the applause continued. He went for a mild nod, an acknowledgment he had often witnessed Her

Supreme-ness perform, and then he wondered what to do next. No BBC sitcom had prepared him for this.

"Keep moving downwards!" shouted an Operator from his earpiece.

The crowd looked up expectantly: Who had organized this surprise and why? Moreover, what amazing magic would this golden statue do next?

"Pete, the coordinates you need are three degrees sideways and at least eight feet down."

No reply.

"You need to move downwards for us to move you."

"What?" said Pete through a strained smile.

"You need to make your way to the bottom of the scaffolding, you're out of range!"

Pete looked down at the street. It was a long way down and full of not only people but stalls as well. A slight drizzle began, and as Pete lifted his hand to wave, his foot slid on the water; he lost his balance and skidded into the splits, which is nothing to the flexible Pete.

"Oh."

"Aargh."

"*Shit!*"

The music faded out and he looked like he was going to fall; the crowd gasped.

Pete's eyes were on the coordinates at the west of the scaffolding just around the corner and four flights down. He back bent down to the next level and then swung his legs over to follow, like a Russian gymnast performing floor work. His feet lightly touched the bar.

"Oh my God . . ."

"Jesus, Mary Mother of five."

Then he swung his legs apart with his toes grabbing onto the poles, moving into the sort of position that had many of the audience wincing.

"Now, you must move now!" shouted a voice in his ear.

He swung onto the next level.

The crowd applauded.

Pete, balancing precariously on a foot-wide bench, bowed, and before he had time to move to his point of contact, Wham! had started to play.

Pete immediately liked it. *Give 'em a few more moves,* he thought, *what harm could that do?*

Pete moved across the slim bench with turns and twists, finishing with a fast-paced up-and-down splits—one of his specialties. The applause continued. And when he swung across the corner of the building like Spider-Man, the applause was so uplifting he felt like he wanted to stay forever—bugger the mission. He liked being noticed, having an audience; it was way better than being invincible.

"Wake me up before you go," he shouted, and the crowd joined in.

"Listen, golden boy, get to the point or you can kiss your so-called 'log' goodbye," said the third in command. "Hilda will be here any minute."

Pete ignored them; he had decided that Wham! was the best music ever, just perfect for splits and backbends, and the more the audience cheered the faster he moved.

The Operators were getting jittery. Hilda was due anytime, and she would blow a fuse if she saw Pete and his "look at me" spectacle.

"We must keep the masses in the dark and the Earthlings ignorant," was Hilda's motto.

"Hardly that now," said the second in command. "He'll be leaving a calling card if we don't do something soon."

The Operators continued to scramble with their connections and discovered that the steel bar could vibrate the coordinates. Pete's body began to vibrate.

Poof! Boom! Fizzle . . .

He dematerialized, leaving behind just his plugulator dangling from the scaffolding pole.

The DJ (who everyone knew as DJ) was standing close by. DJ noticed the plugulator, picked it up, and put it in his shoulder bag.

"Bollocks," shouted the first in command, "how could we have missed that?"

❄

*H*ilda headed to the kitchen of new cuisine. It was her favorite place to think, taste, and coordinate, or "interfere," as Beryl liked to call it. Unlike Beryl, she had been there many times, even for a while as an apprentice, and had done her fair share of herb-picking—giving cheek was pretty much tattooed into her DNA.

She entered through the back way and was just on the verge of requesting a tasting session when the fridge door, which was as wide as a barn, opened, completely hiding her.

Lidia was describing the vision of a gray-blue beehive passing by to an unconvinced audience of four. Hilda held her breath . . . Beryl was a pure limo lady, never an incognito-walking type. Beryl liked an entrance with a fanfare and a few footmen and got decidedly grumpy when there was no applause. While sneaking about the kitchen, Hilda's eyes flashed across the garden to the shed . . . what was she up to?

"I saw it between those two shelves there," the girl said. "It was gliding by like a UFO looking for a landing place . . ."

"It's a beehive."

"What?"

"Hairstyle from the past."

"No, it was definitely gliding on its own, I didn't see no neck . . . it was from another planet, I tell you, this kitchen is . . . is . . . a landing pad—it's radioactive."

The dark lady laughed. "That's plucking too much fennel that is . . . next time do it in the fresh air." She closed the fridge door and stared at Hilda.

"You want to try our new casserole with pickled beets, although Herself over there calls it a stew."

"Not now," said Hilda and headed for the shed; she was planning to make her "catching them off guard" entrance.

Hilda flashed across the grass like a young paratrooper, running from hedge to stone to hedge, hiding. When she got to the shed, she crouched below the window and was about to make her way to the door when she heard, "*If this gets out, the shit will really hit the proverbial.*"

She stopped.

She slunk to her "incognito viewing spot" (peephole), silently skidding on an empty pizza carton. Hilda, like a pro, caught her breath along with her footing just in time to view Pete disappearing with a *piff*, *puff*, and *poof* of smoke. She held her breath and peered through her viewing spot once more, this time with her magnifying glasses. She saw, on the screen, the replay of Pete's piff-puff-poof exit, and as the smoke cleared there was DJ George, on his knees, looking at the plugulator.

What the sliced beetroot is going on?

She had gone to all the trouble of making sure that Mex's equipment was the worst possible—*including* a B&B leaflet as out-of-date as a coffee machine. And then Her Leadership goes and sends Pete down, a robot with too much knowledge and an incognito pose like no other, a robot that had been caught loitering around her "Magna Carta is a Starter" file; a robot "worth the watching."

She looked again.

Who the pickle gives a robot a plugulator of that caliber? It's top of the line.

Hilda was about to charge into the shed and demand heads for rolling, pay to be cut (except they didn't get any). She was about to throw her weight around, as she was often known to do on Planet Hy Man, when something behind her beating breast told her to wait.

"Zoom in on Woody's coordinates," yelled the voice from the back.

"Yes yes yes, he'll be there soon."

Hilda waited and watched . . .

---

1. *A pose adopted by robots and the masses, helping them to blend into the background, or at least let those of great importance know that they are not worth noticing.*
2. *A by-product of egg popping, and a material like no other. It is so flexible that a robot made of it will never age and finds yoga as easy as the mere blink of an eye.*

    Egg Popping is a recently accepted profession established by the first retired man spy. Eggs (also known as valuable real-estate) from a successful woman can earn her a tidy commission —which Mex was banking on to provide her with a better robot than the damnable Pete.

Chapter Eight

WOODY

"Never kid a kidder; they won't rest until they get you back." – Beryl

Woody, a dwarf with a lot of time on his hands, had spent a lot of it sitting in coffee shops dreaming about his sci-fi novels until the bus shelter incident. Since then he placed his torn camouflaged trousers under his bed, avoided his mum and decided to take the bus everywhere. Just in case . . .

The first bus he took was to the Edinburgh International Book Festival. He went to every workshop on the programme about fantasy, sci-fi, time travel, and anything else that remotely sounded like the sort of thing a story about a porn star shifting dimensions might fit into. And he was almost inspired until he stupidly attended the last workshop of the day: "Is Sci-Fi as Dead as an Albatross or Just Comatose?"

His heart was down; his idea was brilliant. It was inspired by his love of Terry Pratchett novels and based around a bus shelter harboring elderly porn stars from other dimensions saving the world from genetically enhanced tomatoes and the like. And for the last two hours, all he and a hundred other would-be writers had heard from "agents in the know" was that comic sci-fi was as dead as test cricket in South Africa.

Not even a free ticket to an Earnest Ernie (unknown stand-up) had cheered him up.

Woody pondered over his Frappuccino. And was just about to skull the last of it when he heard a loud clatter from the disabled toilet followed by the sound of a hand dryer and muffled, unfamiliar cursing.

Pete had materialized in the disabled toilet stall, hitting his head on the dryer, which didn't improve his mood; he was cheesed off about being ripped from his audience so coldly. One minute he was acrobating like a spider of the highest order and the next, like a flash, he had landed with one foot in the "john" (as Vegas liked to call it) and one on the seat.

It was all too undignified, and cold, to speak of. To make matters worse, because of the complications of his Teflon, Pete had also endured the great discomfort of time travel. It was now eight hours on from his time in Dunoon, eight hours out of his life gone forever, along with his stomach, so it seemed; typical of those damnable Operators, they had no respect for Teflon.

He looked about at the complicated arrangement of pulleys and bars. This was a "john," but not as he knew it. Her Leathership's toilet was a pretty straightforward affair, and cleaning was a mere press of a button. But this was more complicated than the deck in *Star Trek*. *What a pickle,* he thought, *what a great pickled egg of a situation.*

Pete looked about the stark white rooms. What was he to pull for what? He hadn't a clue, so he looked in the mirror above the sink and began to rub his dented face back into shape and nearly tripped. His foot was lodged in the toilet just above the water.

What the gherkin was going on? One minute he's entertaining on an impressive scale, the next he's in a toilet, minutes away from being flushed by God knows what.

He yanked his foot out of the toilet, setting off the flushing of "blue water," and the hand dryer revved up again. He then gave his leg a good shake, which set off the hand dryer yet again. Then, being a robot of great imagination, he thrust his leg under the hand dryer. But, also being a robot who had materialized, dematerialized, and materialized again, his spirit level was all over the place, and he began to see double. Pete tripped and grabbed the nearest thing to hand, which happened to be the emergency cord.

*W*oody watched as the staff gathered around the door now blocked by Pete. The assistant manager knocked on the door while the others shouted.

"Anything wrong?"

"You okay in there?"

"Can you let us in?"

The staff looked at Woody; he knew what they wanted. It wasn't the first time he had been asked to squeeze through a window the size of a cat flap. He sighed.

"Extra coffee and any amount of cake," said the assistant manager.

Woody said nothing, just left his almost-finished Frappuccino and edged himself through the window. He jumped down onto the floor and bent over Pete, whom he assumed was on the piss.

*H*ilda watched. Through her peephole she could see the two large screens monitored by the Operators.

Woody landed on the toilet floor like a cat, sending the Operators into a frenzy of sighing. They watched the landing a few more times.

"He must be what, all of four foot three inches?" said the third in command.

"If that," said another.

"He can land, that's for sure . . ."

Short had always been the new tall in Planet Hy Man, ever since the overthrow of men and all their sports equipment. Nowadays a man with few words and stature below five feet was a god to all but Beryl. Beryl didn't believe in gods, unless you counted her latest hairdresser.

Hilda smiled to herself. *This Woody—he could be a godsend.* Silently she left, like a bat fluttering in the dark, making a mental note to get the footman around to clear up the pizza boxes.

Chapter Nine

COSTA COFFEE

"Seeing is believing, but tasting is even better." –Pete's log

Woody looked at the crumpled, gold-colored body lying on the toilet floor and assumed that he was a very posh street performer. A first for Woody; the bodies he usually found on the floor were homeless and a bit grubby. Pete was not only immaculate but he had no body odor, not even a hint of pee.

Woody stepped closer and gently shook Pete's shoulder.

"Wake me up before you go go . . ." muttered Pete.

Woody shook his shoulder again. "You cannae sleep here."

"Captain's Log; Stargate . . . 219 AD . . . err. What?"

"You need to get up."

Pete rubbed the side of his head and muttered, "Huh?" He opened his eyes and stared at Woody as his face blurred from one to two and back again.

"Come on, mister, you cannae sleep here."

Pete was about to ask what a "cannae" was, but he decided to wait until Woody's face remained still before he said anything.

※

*B*eryl looked at her latest updates as they flashed up on her super-deluxe, high-definition, extra-slim stationary H-Pad screen. It was next year's model, hidden in her bedroom for *testing* purposes, with a new experimental fourth smelling dimension, which first thing in the morning before a coffee was not always advisable.

"Reporting to her Supreme-ness; it's official, landing has occurred. Pete assisted out of his arrival pad by Woody. Pete saw two Woodys blend into one, over and out, Stargate."

"Woody?" shouted Beryl. "Why is Woody still present and what's with the Stargate? I thought that went out with roll-on deodorant."

"Deodorant, ma'am?"

*T*he Operators were in a pickle. The plugulator was in the hands of some male who could probably read, and it was their fault.

"Stalling is all we can do," said the second in command. "If it gets out what's saved on those files . . . our jobs, all this"—she gestured to the darkened shed and the paper cups of watered-down beverage—"will be gone."

"So what?" muttered a few.

"So what? Do you want to go back to your old jobs?"

"I didn't have one."

"Me neither."

The room fell silent.

"Because if we don't find a way of downloading Pete's files incognito, those above will . . ." The second in command downed her weak tea with distaste. "Actually, I have no idea what they will do . . . but I am sure if they knew how we helped Pete download, it would not be pleasant."

"I'd do it again in a flash," shouted the voice from the back.

"Me too," shouted another.

"Yes, thank you, comrades," said the first in command, pulling the cup from her deputy, "but I am sure that won't be necessary being that he is now on Earth."

*W*oody helped Pete up without mentioning the wet foot or the small indent on Pete's face that was slowly puffing back into place. Pete again looked in the mirror, gave his face a rub, and smiled at the handsome man.

Woody then brushed some toilet paper from Pete's shoulder and noticed something funny about him. Sure, he was painted gold, but his shoulder felt padded, soft, and nothing like leather.

*"P*ete landed in the john and is now in crash mode" flashed up on Beryl's H-Pad.

"I thought he was swinging from a scaffold," shouted Beryl.

"He was, Your Sirness, but now he is anything but, swinging in a john, and has been bashed into clueless mode . . ."

Beryl was speechless.

❋

*W*oody introduced himself and then asked Pete for his name as he helped Pete from the toilet. Pete said nothing but watched as Woody stood up—his height hardly altered. Woody's head looked like it belonged to a bigger body.

Pete was silenced by the beauty of such a man. Pete felt he was in the presence of a very important and desirable man, something that had not been seen on Planet Hy Man in decades . . . well, at least not since before Pete's time, anyway.

It was then, as he rubbed his head for the second time, that he realized his plugulator was gone. He began to look around as Woody started to make "you need to move out of here" noises.

Woody walked Pete outside onto the street and left him there.

Pete had no idea where he was or what time it was, and he had lost his plugulator. Who was going to mind his back now?

Pete had worked hard to make connections with Operators from the day he started his placement with Her Leathership. While Herself was up there—in the chambers, making "let's not forget the man spy" petitions—he was in the shed, giving lighting advice and bringing creamy cappuccinos to the Operators, while they updated his plugulator with more storage space than . . . an IBM backup plant. What was he going to do now?

Pete watched Woody head back into the shop. He didn't want him to go. Pete liked Woody's face; it was warm, intelligent, and sympathetic. The sort of face that anyone alone and lost would cling to. Pete squelched back into the café. No one noticed—the staff were in the kitchen and the only customer apart from Woody was a very old lady standing at the counter, and her eyesight was so bad she thought she was in the library.

Pete inhaled the aroma of coffee and made his way to Woody's table. He felt a rumbling in his stomach, something he had never felt before. He gestured toward the plate of flapjacks, some covered in white and dark chocolate.

"Is this all yours?" he said.

Woody said nothing but gestured for Pete to join him. He watched Pete pull up a chair with curiosity. Pete appeared too polite to be Scottish, too white to be a migrant, and too curious to be English—he was unplaceable.

"So, this establishment; it serves coffee?" said Pete.

Woody looked at him: "It's called a coffee shop."

Pete mumbled something about *too good to be true* as he picked up a sugar packet, surveyed it, and then shook it close to his ear like it was some sort of musical instrument. He shook it harder, until the sugar packet broke and sugar went everywhere.

Woody laughed, and then so did Pete.

"May I?" Pete gestured toward a flapjack of high quality.

"Sure, knock yourself out," said Woody.

Pete turned the slice in his hand and sniffed it. "Apricot, I gather, and"—he sniffed again—"condensed milk. I have heard about this but yet . . . nothing can capture the true fragrance . . ."

"Some people just eat it," said Woody.

Pete took a bite of the flapjack; golden syrup and creamy milky taste hit his mouth like an explosion of sweetness he knew nothing about and had never experienced before. He bit down on the oats and as they crunched into his jaw he sighed. "So this is what a mouth is really for," he murmured.

"Some would say," said the assistant manager, walking by. He stopped at the table. "That is a flapjack that holds its own. You can go too far with a flapjack, but this little baby balances it just right."

Pete took another bite; this time apricot hit the side of his mouth, setting off a tingling sensation that caused him to drool—another new and mildly disconcerting sensation.

The assistant manager stood in awe; this man was a true connoisseur of the finer things, a man with taste, despite his getup. "It is something to savor, is it not?"

"Yes, siree."

"It's just a flapjack," said Woody.

Chapter Ten

SATIN AND SILK

"A chandelier by any other name still swings both ways." —a Voted In unknown

Beryl took a sip of the illegal beverage and stretched out on her bed wrapped in her favorite black satin sleeping gown; it was shiny, expensive, and as hard-to-get as shoes for a footman. It slid across her fingers like oil.

It was a warm morning, and she had the windows open with her silk curtains billowing. Normally by now she would have looked in one of the many mirrors in her bedroom, caught her reflection, and wondered at what ruling had done to her looks.

Beryl was young when she took over the leadership. It was back in the fifties when there were still a few men around, but they were aging fast. Once women discovered how to reproduce without a man, it was all downhill for the men, and they began to wither. They had little purpose. They did try various rebellions—there was the famous arm-wrestling treaty and the revolt of the cyclist—but no one took them seriously, even the robots.

In the end, most men gave in and resigned themselves to the gym . . .

Those were the days, when she had a face worth photographing and a blue rinse worked a treat. Now everything was complicated.

Even the Operators were questioning her, and they used to be so . . . manageable.

She opened her manifesto, picked up her pen, and rolled it between her finger and thumb. She usually wrote freestyle, as she liked the feel of a pen dipped in ink and the rustle of a turned page. She also knew that no one, not even the Voted In, used paper and pen. Her manifesto was safe, a secret, and she could write whatever she wanted. But this morning she couldn't think, let alone write.

She flicked through the pages and stopped at an entry from a few months ago—*"Hilda snorts like a pig and walks like one too"*—and took another sip.

That woman has poked her nose into every suggestion—objected, questioned, and poured scorn onto every one of my amendments. She is like one of those annoying, smart-arsed, sniveling younger brothers that—thank God—don't exist anymore.

Today she exceeded herself; she stood under that ridiculous penis-shaped chandelier reading from her surveys—in a trench coat. She looked like Inspector Gadget reading out his shopping list. And all I could think of was . . . well . . . men, hot dogs, and those god awful speeches they used to make.

"Have we not progressed?" I asked.

No one said anything; they just looked at me like I was speaking gibberish. Apparently, the Operators are to be taken seriously and I am not! After all, they are the ones who filled in all those damn surveys . . .

And then, right in the middle of the "let's freeze the finance" presentation, the recording froze as they, the Operators, left for their "whatever" with "whoever", okay-ed by you-know-who, she in the trench coat. And I was left with a viewing screen as impotent as a footman.

"Give it a good bash," shouted Vegas.

That's their answer to everything . . . as if a good bash is going to do anything other than give the basher a sore hand.

"We are working with top-of-the-range equipment that has connections to the White House, the Kremlin, any parliament you can swing a cat at, and BBC reruns. Do you really think a good bash is what is needed here?" I said.

And did they listen? I may as well have read a shopping list to a man in a porn shop.

Beryl let out one of her long, elegant sighs . . .

All the signs were there: she was losing control, and Hilda was behind everything. Why hadn't she seen it earlier?

Beryl poured herself another coffee, this time with extra cream, and stared out through her patio window as the sun rose. Hilda had called the mission a waste of oxygen. If only she knew how close they were to lights-out—a few months, maybe a year, depending how extravagant the Voted In were. She sighed and cursed Legless.

The same morning Beryl was contemplating the aging process, Hilda was in the shed—yet again stirring things up. Hilda, buoyed up on the kitchen of new cuisine's latest stew/casserole, waltzed into the shed and demanded to know who was the pint-size male—catching them off guard before pre-breakfast tea.

"He's a coffee addict," said the second in command.

"Unemployed," said another in command, but what level no one knew.

"His mother's a hoot," said the first in command.

"He goes to a Starbucks every day and writes," piped up a small voice at the back.

Hilda held up her hands for the others to stop. "Follow that dwarf," she shouted, "and keep me informed." Which was code for don't tell Beryl. And then she strode outside the shed like the captain of a ship heading into battle, ready for her second portion of stew.

Hilda had a thing for power dressing; from the day she left the Operators' shed, she cut her hair and took to wearing extra-large suits rather than the trim-fitting tuxedo. She was a woman who advocated swimming in cold water and eating sauerkraut and beetroot, stating that if it was good for athletes of the north it was good for her. Her stride was on par with the Kremlin march.

Later, Hilda, still in striding mode, headed to the Voted In beverage room—the smell of pizza hit her and she smiled. Pizza was expensive and banned from meetings by Beryl.

"Wouldn't it be a hoot," said Hilda, "to follow Woody?"

A few of the Voted In dropped their pizza in mid bite.

"I mean, Woody is a bonus. He could be of help to us here, make our job that much easier."

No one really got the "much easier" line. However, no one argued; watching Woody was better than any cappuccino or foot rub.

Two hours later, Beryl had called a meeting.

Chapter Eleven

BERYL

"Give with one hand and tax with the other." –Manifesto the Great, 1955

Beryl ordered, "Stop now," and the screen flickered, crackled, then slid into a slit in the ceiling.

"Will that be all, Sirness?" said a soothing voice from the screen.

Beryl nodded as the Voted In wondered what was next. They had spent the afternoon watching the plight of Pete in a Starbucks disabled toilet while listening to Beryl talk about the futility of poor coordinates and the cost of mistakes. She even threw in her "serious threat to the planet's invisibility speech." It was a relentless experience, which no amount of coffee could make bearable.

"Shall we watch Woody again?" said a small voice from the back. "Maybe just the end bit where he climbs in . . ."

Beryl glared as the Voted In exchanged looks.

One of the footmen passed over the amended minutes in a messenger.

"Is this the fourth or fifth amendment?" Beryl asked as the messenger was passed around the table. No one answered. It was, after all, an appeal to cover the extra cost of Pete's telespray [1]balls-up. Each Voted In had to read the messenger before Beryl did, and if they amended it, they had to explain why. It was a process Hilda liked to skip and a process Beryl insisted upon.

The Voted In passed the messenger from one to another until it landed in front of Vegas. She pulled at the seal and looked about the table for help; a few shrugged. Vegas, frustrated, pulled at a corner with her teeth. Beryl nodded to a footman, who picked up the messenger and placed it into Beryl's outstretched hand. Beryl lifted a nail file from her pocket.

"The reconstruction of Teflon-ic leather is expensive, especially when completed on another planet," Beryl said with an expert twist of her file. "I mean, robots landing in bathroom stalls? Whatever next, fishing with whips?"

A few of the Voted In chuckled as Beryl swiftly manipulated the seal with an impressive command of her nail file; several blank sheets floated into the air; the Voted In stared—waiting for the minutes to appear.

"I mean, whose idea was it to telespray him into a coffee shop, for beetroot sake?" said Beryl.

No one said anything, as it was, after all, Hilda's idea. And pleasing Hilda was safer than not.

"Look," snapped Beryl. "Can you tell me if this is a setup? And if it is, we need to nip it in the . . . proverbial . . ."

Beryl waited for an answer, and when none came she tried another tact: "And what of this man of limited stature?"

"Woody," said the voice from the back.

"Yes," said Beryl.

"He is considered to be of service," said Vegas.

"Oh, by whom?" said Beryl.

Silence.

"Can anyone tell me why, then?"

Still no answer.

"Well," said Beryl. "This Woody is bad for morale—every time his name is mentioned you lot act like teenagers. What's wrong with you?"

"Woody is the only thing decent about this whole saga."

"He's short."

"And kind."

"Don't forget funny . . ."

"Exactly. Short, kind, and funny—how many times does that happen in one man?"

"And he knows a thing or two about flapjacks," said the voice from the back.

"Everyone knows about flapjacks."

Beryl shouted over the rabble, "He seems to have an influence over Pete, probably reads his mind . . . which could cause trouble . . ."

"Thought that was just the Identities," said Vegas.

Beryl sighed. She could be home on her silk sheets getting a little caffeine blast[2]. Instead she was fighting on all fronts and Hilda was not even present. Ever since the story of Legless's death had surfaced, the Voted In had lost interest—the Identities it seemed were no longer of any importance, let alone a threat. In fact, Beryl was sure the only reason they agreed to the mission was to free up Mex's flat. Vegas had been spotted loitering around Mex's balcony measuring things up like an undertaker.

Beryl did her best; she talked about how the Identities inspired by *Star Trek* and heaven knows what else are to be not only watched but stopped at all cost. "I mean," she said, "there is talk of the Identities building a spaceship, which could cause us grievous planetary harm . . . we must be vigilant."

"*Star Trek*, Captain Kirk—they are as believable as a footman's wig," said Hilda, appearing in the doorway. The minutes, still suspended in the air unread, *poofed* into confetti and fluttered onto the table.

Hilda in her spy trench coat strutted into the room clutching her LEADER KNOWS BEST mug. She laughed (or snorted, as Beryl liked to call it). "You really are ridiculous, Beryl," she said.

"The internet," continued Beryl, "has opened a nest of hornets."

The Voted In exchanged looks; no one spoke of the obvious, that the internet made their life easy. The microchip gave Operators access to phones, tablets, iPads, even surveillance cameras—in fact, anything microchipped Microsoft-ed or Apple-Mac-ed and even, if bored, a bit of Kindle. Watching Earth was as easy as opening the screen and shouting *play*. Who would want the good old days back, viewing Earth through mirrors—how *rubbish* was that? The lighting, the timing, looking at the world through toothpaste-splattered bathroom mirrors . . .

"I like the hornets' nest," shouted the voice from the back.

Everyone looked.

"I mean the internet."

"Yes, well . . . the Identities talk of rediscovering their roots, and when they do, the hornets' nest," said Beryl with a glare at the back, "will be well and truly trampled."

"A serious threat to the invisibility of Planet Hy Man," yelled Hilda. "I find that hard to believe; they can't even read a book let alone figure out how to search for their 'roots.' The idea that they would manage a mission is laughable."

Hilda was so loud that even the footmen outside the Voted In room and the Operators in the shed out the back could hear.

"The Identities will be the end of us," Beryl muttered, but nobody listened. She looked about the blank faces . . . *It'd be easier to push a weasel through a cat flap than raise interest, from this lot.*

Beryl, with a dispirited sigh, watched the confetti dissolve on the table. Some days she wondered whether it was all worth it.

*H*ilda stretched out on her bed, wrapped in her favorite black satin sleeping gown. It was a cool evening after a hot day, and she had the windows open with her silk curtains billowing.

She took a sip of the illegal beverage and looked at one of the many mirrors in her bedroom. Her lips tilted a little to the left as she adjusted her black robe; it was just like Beryl's except newer, and silkier. Hilda couldn't resist looking in a mirror. She had a leader's face with a great Roman nose, worthy of at least one decent portrait hanging above the "chair gallery."

Hilda let out one of her robust Russian groans.

I must keep an eye on every movement, keep control, convince the Voted In that Beryl is a threat as real as a footman's inability to think, stand, and answer at the same time.

Hilda poured herself another coffee, this time with extra cream,

and stared out the window onto her patio. It was a clear night and the
Milky Way was on view. Hilda wondered: How long would it all take?

------

1. *Inspired by Planet Hy Man's first truly scientific woman who had a crush on Star Trek's
   Captain Kirk. She was an enthusiastic shower-maker who designed a power shower so strong
   it moved women from inside the shower to outside—she saw the potential.*

   *For a while it was all the rage for the Voted In as they telesprayed from one shop to the
   next, frightening shop assistants until the shop assistants rebelled and started charging startle
   charges.*
2. *Coffee on Planet Hy Man is for the elite and was introduced mainly to keep the Voted In
   awake during meetings.*

Chapter Twelve

LEATHER

"Leather is as leather does." —Anon, door of the shed

Mex sat on the bed. She was starving. She looked about the room. It was dark with seventies wallpaper she recognized from the sitcoms that she and Pete watched together, the sort of sitcoms that had Pete muttering mirth-like noises and Mex wondering why.

Her mood was not good, for not only was her stomach rumbling like a thunderstorm, but the Voted In had made a complete pickled egg of the arrival. They had sent Pete to some town she had never heard of, and before she could find out where, he was telesprayed again. And now, thanks to her bargain-basement equipment, she could no longer find his coordinates. Rather, she was expected to "lay low" and wait for him to contact her—a robot who got upset about an anniversary card.

Mex sighed, opened her backpack onto the candlewick bedspread, and pulled out her H-Pad. It was bleeping furiously; Beryl was waiting. Mex typed a message . . .

"Women are treated with great familiarity here. They wear clothes unbefitting of the weather and shoes of great height, allowing water in. Running is obviously not respected on Earth."

She pressed second-class send. Her H-Pad had, on Earth, leaked energy like a tennis racket under a tap and Mex had to conserve as much as possible. She needed Pete here to recharge it—not an easy feat when she needed her H-Pad to find Pete.

She stared at herself in the mirror. Her weapons of intuitions were shot. She felt nothing, smelt zero, and had as much idea of what to do as a footman. On Planet Hy Man, intuition pumped through Mex's veins like air through a foot pump. Once Mex had the scent of someone, she could trace them from miles away. She was like a bloodhound, like a shark on the scent of a bleeding seal—except she was a vegetarian.

On Planet Hy Man, Mex had a body that could heal in seconds, the heart of a woman that had never loved or wanted to, and the mother of all intuitions. Mex had been designed, educated, and brought up to protect her mother planet. She was the ultimate spying machine, the best man spy ever.

Mex had spent a lifetime scouting for hidden men. At first it was a challenge. The men were young and virile; they hid in places that took days to find and, once found, put up a pretty decent fight. Back then Mex was young, the top of the pile, the pick of the litter, and she could source men that no one else could. And her reputation grew, so much so that the mere mention of her name had men surrendering from their sheds like something out of a western; except there were no guns —just herself, wielding her whip around like a circus lion tamer.

Of course, as the men grew older, their hiding places became obvious. Broom cupboards and abandoned cars, some even dressed as women—*so predictable*. Finally, the men stopped fighting and started handing themselves in for the plush footman jobs.

And it was all thanks to her.

Her future was looking good: resting on her famous reputation was the promise of a new, better life. She was "this close" to a pension of double figures and "even closer" to her penthouse on the seaside block with its patio and fragrant view and, thanks to her reputation, she could make a fortune egg popping. The eggs of someone like her were worth a fortune to the baby clinic.

Granted there were a few hiccups, but as long as she kept reminding those in power of how much the planet owed to the man spy fraternity . . . the fraternity wouldn't be forgotten. But now, thanks to this pickled egg of a mission, her penthouse by the sea was as far away from her as Pete and his plugulator. And as for her reputation—it went down the tubes the day she left the planet for Earth, worthless as her eggs would soon be. And the fraternity—without her would they still keep up the pressure, keep the memory alive?

Her H-Pad began to bleep again; this time it was Pete. His face appeared on her screen with an unrecognizable look. She scrambled with the volume, shouted "Pete" several times, and watched as the picture faded away. If Mex knew what swearing was, she would have said a mouthful. Instead she tossed the H-Pad onto the bed and stared at the ceiling.

*M*ex's mind raced back to the week before, when she tried with all her might to argue against going down to Earth.

That night, after listening for what seemed like the hundredth time to stories of how good the food was *"down there"* from not only Pete but anyone else she asked, Mex could not take any more. She—after her nightcap—raced up to Beryl's pad prepared with every argument under the Milky Way. And for a while Mex thought she had won Beryl over, had her reaching for the "retrieve a plan" button. Without interruption Beryl listened, nodded, and smiled until Mex had exhausted all arguments. Then Beryl closed her curtains, pushed a creamy macchiato Mex's way, and told her *the Story*.

Beryl knew her prodigy like the back of an H-Pad. She knew that Mex would probably try something coercive like coming around with a nightcap, and she was ready.

"It was a hedge like no other," said Beryl. "It was 1959, I remember it well . . ."

Mex held her breath. She could handle it . . .

Telling *the Story* was way worse than the watching of *the Story*, and telling *the Story* to a woman of intuition like Mex was on a par with a rollercoaster ride with vertigo. Mex's imagination was in 3-D and long lasting. If she pictured it, she experienced it—not always a talent one would want.

"On a hot afternoon, while huddled behind a hedge, Legless caught a glimpse of a woman in an apron and fluffy slippers."

Mex started to gag . . . it was just a matter of sentences.

"As she bent over her basket of washing, Legless stared at her small behind pressed against her nylon skirt and lust filled his loins."

"Stop, stop—I will go, please, no more . . ."

Mex sighed. *God, I am weak.*

Three sentences, that was all it took, three, and not only was she shouting "stop, stop, I will go," but vowing that she would "never look at another hedge again." And what made it worse was goddamn Pete with his smug "I give you two paragraphs" comment; she didn't even make it to the end of the first.

She heard a "*Star Trek* at your service" from the H-Pad and knew before she even looked that it was Pete using his hammy American accent. Pete waved at Mex. He had the glazed expression of happiness mixed with the discomfort of indigestion; his latte had gone down the wrong way.

He belched.

Pete had tucked into more cakes than a dieter on the rebound. Pete had eaten cakes like he had never eaten before, which he hadn't. And as the sugar and caffeine hit his virgin system, he felt a surge of pleasure. Pete was on a high, something he had never heard of let alone felt.

He glanced across at the explosion of colored sugar before him, wondering what to try next. He tapped the cherry perched on top of the frosting. *Do I lick or bite?*

Woody lifted his Nokia from his pocket and was about to let his mum know he'd be late when Pete, with all thoughts of being incognito lost under a sea of sugar and caffeine, grabbed the phone. His vision was blurred, his hands were a little shaky, but he hadn't seen one of these since . . . the gym days.

He began to press things. Just wait till the others in the yoga class saw what he was tucking into.

Woody watched Pete click, push, flip, flatten, and fizzle the mobile as he tried to tune it in to Planet Hy Man frequency. Woody knew when to ask and when not to. And he also knew that Pete was as high as a jumbo jet and had no idea how to take a photograph.

"Oh, bugger and beetroot!"

"Here, let me," said Woody.

The Voted In sighed; they watched Woody direct Pete to the window to catch the light. They watched Woody maneuver Pete into the best position for a photo as Pete insisted on "getting the cakes in too."

"Woody is the be-all and end-all," said one Voted In as the others sighed.

Woody handed the phone back to Pete as Mex's face appeared on the small screen, her face packed like a sardine against the sides, thanks to being a coordinate or two out.

"Pete's log; Captain Kirk," Pete said and then snorted at his own wit.

"Pete?"

"Yes sirree, ma'am."

"We haven't much time," she said.

Pete let out another belch along with a "pardon me, ma'am."

"Is that a coffee? Are you in a coffee shop?"

"Ma'am, it's what is known around these parts as a skinny latté."

"Quickly, Pete—your coordinates."

"I am at a superb coffee establishment with a nicely compact young man by the name of Woody. He's coming back to . . . reconvene with us." Pete pointed the mobile at Woody; Woody gave an embarrassed wave.

"And me," shouted the elderly lady at the counter.

"Coordinates, Pete," she shouted as Pete's face came in and out of focus. She gave her H-Pad a good bash on the wooden headboard. The

H-Pad groaned and gave her a mouthful about headaches, communication, and the requirement of a clear head when communicating.

"We're close by," Pete sniggered. "Depending of course on what you call close."

"Would you just read me your coordinates and cut the comedian jargon—what's wrong with you?"

"Woody. Why, ma'am, he is an absolute scream with the waitress."

"Assistant manager," shouted the assistant manager.

"And he knows all about coffee, not only with milk but with toffee, caramel, and marshmallows."

"Connections, Pete." Mex stared into the fuzzy picture on the H-Pad. She noticed the empty coffee cups on the table. *How many had he had?*

Pete, high on sugar, laughed. "Who needs a plugulator when you have a pal like Woody," he shouted into the Nokia.

"What? Plugulator? What the pickled egg has happened to your plugulator?"

Pete tapped the side of his nose, which annoyed not only Mex but also Woody.

Mex stared at Pete's image as it fizzled in and out of view with an "oh bugger and pickled egg" from Pete as the H-Pad spat, crackled, and then completely died. Mex watched Pete's face fade from view and cursed every single damnable Voted In.

While she was making do with a last-century rechargeable appliance that couldn't even last a journey, let alone a night, they, the Voted In, were making decisions with their fancy, extra-large deluxe screen with sensory sound.

A higher-quality H-Pad would never need recharging.

"I am heading for the café, don't move," she shouted at the blank screen, knowing that the only being who heard was probably the barking dog next door.

She knew she needed to get there soon; she had no idea how many coffees Pete had had, but what she did know was that he was now a liability. The most she could hope for was that a high Pete was incoherent to the masses and performing his famous splits instead of talking.

Mex jumped to attention, poised for action—just what sort of action, she had no idea. She knew she should run because that's what she always did, but where? She put on her leather jacket, adjusted her belt, and then swore. What was the goddamn point of a belt with a flat H-Pad? She readjusted her jacket and looked in the mirror.

Incognito or obvious as a footman's wig?

Mex sighed, she looked nothing like the women she saw last night or even, heaven forbid, like Bunnie and her "whatever" outfit. She was supposed to know what to do instinctively and she couldn't even make up her mind about her jacket, let alone a belt. What was wrong with her? Pete was in a café somewhere; and she was still staring at her own reflection.

Now she had no choice—she had to soldier on in this godforsaken place, with or without her great talent; *maybe after a few runs I'll pick up the scent,* she thought as she headed into the passageway.

She walked past the glass cabinet and Bunnie's head peered from a door marked private.

"You heading out?" Bunnie asked over the barking of a dog.

Mex stared at Bunnie's round face. It was a pleasant, friendly face, and Mex lingered.

Bunnie opened the door wider, revealing a flowery dressing gown along with the faint whiff of something unfamiliar. Then a squirrel of a dog pushed the door open and raced out to sniff Mex.

"You wanting a coffee?" Bunnie said—she was desperate to try out her new range of Nescafé Gold Skinny Cappuccino sachets.

Mex's hand casually strayed onto the dog's head; she looked at her reflection in the mirror beside the glass cabinet. *I'm as incognito as a fish on a bench and as obvious as one of Pete's jokes in the refreshment rooms.*

"Bunnie," she said. "Does this jacket work?"

Chapter Thirteen

BUNNIE'S BUSINESS

"A dog by any other name still needs a walk." –Bunnie's favorite saying

Bunnie asked Mex into the inner sanctum, as she called it, the place where no one was allowed, even (according to Bunnie) Don the cabbie. Mex followed.

The room was small, white, and sparse—nothing like Mex's green and orange room, or like the plush red velvet decor of the hallway. It was pure-looking with bare walls, apart from a couple of large corkboards full of snapshots of people, each with a rating underneath, either a smiling or a sad face, and arrows crossing from one photo to another.

"I like making people happy," Bunnie said.

Mex looked confused.

"I pair people up."

Mex still looked confused.

"I am a matchmaker."

Mex, who was staring at the photographs, mumbled something about "a lot of men" and then began to count them—*they all wanted a match?*

"Used to make a packet once, not now, romance is not as profitable —but easier than other things . . ."

Mex continued to stare at Bunnie's photographs: it was true what they said about Earth women. *They wanted partners? How crazy!*

"Aye, things aren't what they used to be; people want the impossible now," said Bunnie. She sighed. "It's a living."

Mex counted the men. *Forty-one, forty-two—unbelievable.*

"When I started, it was just blowjobs and flavored condoms, so easy. I brought up all three of my kids with those takings . . . one's a doctor *of sorts*, another's in India discovering the inner child, and the other has three children, *of sorts*."

Mex noticed some women were paired with other women and some men with other men—she was now completely confused.

"Aye, it's all changed now, not what it used to be. Now it's all water-works and waxing—God, the waxing. In my day, body hair was a thing of celebration, men loved a bit of pubic; now it's wax this and wax that. After a trip to the salon you can't even walk straight, it's like having a Brillo Pad between your legs."

Bunnie began to snigger—that was always her favorite joke.

"Now everything is larger than life and gravity defying, the internet has seen to that. I ask you, since when has . . ." She turned to Mex—whose face had the expression of a kitten staring for the first time at a fire, spellbound, engrossed and desperate to touch.

She hasn't a clue, thought Bunnie.

Bunnie watched Mex finger a photograph; she knew there was something weird about Mex from the moment she saw her whip waving like a cat's tail behind her.

Sheila from Bombay—*as if.*

Of course, Mex talking like the Queen after a serious bit of drilling from the dentist did arouse suspicion—that and the fact that when Bunnie mentioned "Coronation Street" as a sort of quick test, Mex looked blank. That really set the hairs on the back of Bunnie's neck on end, as erect as one of her satisfied customers . . .

Bunnie eyed Mex's trim figure. *Everyone knows what* Corrie *is, don't they?*

Bunnie was curious, a feeling she hadn't felt in a long time. And she was even more curious when Izzie her dog wrapped herself around Mex's leg, and Mex, still with the look of a kitten, bent to stroke.

Mex's backpack fell from her shoulders and, just like Woody's had, the contents scattered across the floor. Mex, engrossed in the delicious feeling of soft fur on her fingers, didn't notice.

Bunnie stared at the contents from Mex's bag: Terry Pratchett, an out-of-date B&B brochure, and a child's iPad—extra-large.

Bunnie picked it up; it weighed a ton. She flipped it about and the H-Pad started to make noises like a man drowning.

"What sort of toy is this?" she said.

Mex continued to pat Izzie.

"I mean, what's all that moaning for?"

Bunnie pressed the buttons—nothing happened. *Maybe it needs charging?*

She looked at Mex, who was now on the floor rubbing Izzie's tummy—*a dog that would have the hand of a postman in a minute*. "Who's a pretty thing," cooed Mex.

Bunnie walked to her "stash drawer" and pulled out a handful of chargers left behind by some of her many visitors. She began to untangle them with an eye still on Mex, Izzie on her lap.

Each charger fitted, even the charger designed for the cigarette lighter in a car. The socket on the H-Pad, like putty, molded itself to whatever Bunnie pushed in and Bunnie, like a child, couldn't resist trying them all. She worked her way through each charger until finally the drowning-man noises stopped.

"*Enough*" flashed on the screen. Bunnie took the hint and plugged it in. The H-Pad purred as the lights flickered on . . .

"Well, I never," said Bunnie.

*B*eryl was frustrated. She was cut off from Mex, a new and very unpleasant experience.

Beryl always saw Mex as a loyal supporter and a great man spy, though Beryl never let on. In fact, Beryl hid her feelings, so well that many often wondered if Beryl had a grudge against Mex. Sometimes Beryl was so cold to Mex that even Hilda felt sorry for her. But Beryl, underneath her tight-lipped commands, had the utmost faith in Mex's talents, even if Mex's incognito name (Sheila) was as incognito as a packet of crisps eaten in the dark.

Beryl arrived at her chambers that morning feeling perturbed. She had decided to fight back and beat them at their own game. She wasn't sure who was playing what with whom, but there was one way of finding out: the beverage room. The Voted In were always in good spirits there.

Beryl walked in as they were experimenting with their new Moroccan spice blend.

They stopped mid plunge and stared. Beryl had never entered the beverage room before. Drinking caffeine with others was not something she liked to do, even in the early days. It was the small talk; Beryl never knew what to say past "how are you?" and "pass the milk."

Beryl, over the frothing of milk, muttered a "greetings."

She talked in her best "I am your safest bet" voice about how she had watched "our Mex" "trek into the bowels of Glasgow—while Pete languished in a Starbucks nowhere near the proposed coordinates," and asked, "why?"

The milk frother looked up. "It was you who sent our esteemed man spy, not us."

"And Pete," said another, "is hardly languishing."

Hilda appeared. She leant against the doorframe with her trench coat tight around her waist and a "this'll be good" smirk on her face. Beryl with her back to the door didn't notice.

"And this Woody," said Beryl. "Why are we still following him?"

"It was all her idea," said the voice by the sink, nodding to Hilda. One of the others flicked her with a tea towel.

Beryl turned and started. Hilda held her gaze, her square frame wedged in the entrance like a tombstone.

"And that's another thing," said Beryl, "this . . . charging up on Earth . . ."

Hilda pulled a here-we-go-again face.

"You should be ashamed of yourself."

"Hear, hear," said the voice by the sink.

"I mean, this theory of yours—"

"Theory?"

"That Earth's atmosphere *just loves* our batteries."

Hilda's immaculate hair didn't flicker once: "Oh, that."

"Yes, that."

Hilda let out a small chuckle as she strode further into the kitchen. No one said a word as her square heels clicked on the marbled floor— even the milk frothing stopped. "Beryl's making a drama out of nothing."

"It is a load of pickled eggs," said Beryl.

"Really?"

"Yes."

"I don't think so."

"Well, I do."

"Really?"

"Yes. Really."

"Surely not. I mean, can it be that difficult to charge things up—to acclimatize to Earth and all its pollution?" Hilda gestured to Beryl. "Perhaps it is you who should be ashamed of yourself."

She looked around the room, making eye contact with all who had the gumption to face her, while Beryl stared at the cleaning roster over the sink.

"How long does it take to *juice up* an H-Pad?" said Hilda.

Silence.

"Anyone?"

"She has to find one first," muttered the voice by the sink.

"What?"

"A juicer."

"Juicing up," said Hilda, "is merely a figure of speech."

Beryl sighed. *Why did I believe her—Miss Know-It-All from nowhere special? Trying to outsmart Hilda was as impossible as keeping the attention of a footman.*

Chapter Fourteen

A WOMAN'S BEST FRIEND

"A bark is never worse than a bite." —Bunnie's second-favorite saying

Mex, with Izzie under one arm and a toastie in the other hand, started to rearrange the photos—the same photos Bunnie had spent all morning working on—and she was getting grease everywhere.

Bunnie pulled another photo from the bin. Izzie barked.

The H-Pad had been charging up for just over three hours, and in that time Mex had demolished three cheese and onion toasties, told Izzie about her arrival on Earth—which didn't take long, detail was not Mex's strong point—and rearranged Bunnie's photographs by pretty much tossing out most of the men.

Bunnie was not impressed. "Will you stop with the photos," she snapped. But Mex didn't hear, or didn't want to. She fed a corner of her toastie to Izzie, who licked it, along with Mex's fingers. Bunnie watched, speechless—what was this woman's secret? Izzie had always been so un-pick-up-able.

The H-Pad lit up, flashing green, blue, and then red, followed by a poor-quality fanfare of trumpets, causing Bunnie to jolt.

"*Here ye, here ye,*" said the H-Pad.

"That'll be Herself," said Mex, handing Izzie the rest of her toast. "She does like an entrance."

"Her Leadership is about to address the situation," said the H-Pad.

"You answer," said Mex. "I am busy."

"Busy—how can you be busy?" said the H-Pad.

Bunnie looked from the H-Pad, flashing like a traffic light backwards, and then at Mex.

"Just pick it up," said Mex to Bunnie.

Bunnie, mumbling something about whose house was it, stared into the contraption. Bunnie's plump white face flashed onto the Operator's screen five times bigger than life size, scaring the Operator.

"Who are you?" said the Operator.

"Who the hell are you?" said Bunnie.

Chapter Fifteen

DJ

"Hearing is not believing and believing doesn't always require hearing." —Anon, scribbled under the table in the room with the view

In Dunoon, DJ, who had picked up the plugulator, was confused. He had spent the whole night with the plugulator—or head mic, as he called it—on his head for a laugh. He wore it while he and his two "Wham! impersonator" *pals* wandered from one pub to another singing Wham! songs and taking it in turns to stuff socks down the front of their trousers. And as the night wore on and the pubs closed, DJ and his Wham! pals ended up in the back of a caravan snoring, wrestling, and—in the case of one Wham! man—procreating: with socks on.

"Wham! one" had bumped into his ex and taken her to the caravan. And, as neither had found any replacement for the other, they decided to use the spare room in the caravan to remind them of old times and rocked the old five berth like there was no tomorrow. Well, as much as possible when you're heading into your forties, two stone heavier than you should be, and tanked up on half a dozen ciders, a chicken tikka and the leftovers of two garlic naans.

The second Operator in command, via the plugulator, had watched with way too close a view.

The Operator stared at the door of the spare room as it swung rhythmically open and shut with a bang *in time to the raging wind,* flashing a view of Wham! one's bare arse, also pulsating *to the raging wind*, with his trousers around his ankles. The noises ranged from high-pitched squeals to growls and more while DJ and Wham! two watched reruns of the World Cup—they had seen Wham! one's pulsating arse many times before.

"Come on, yer bastard!"

The sounds and songs were completely unfamiliar to the Operator, and before you could shout "wake me up before you go-go," the Operators had called all her fellow Operators to watch, even those on a break or not due in until tomorrow. And as the room filled, so did the noises they made. By the end of the night, when Wham! two was snoring and Wham! one was trying for a home goal yet again, DJ began to listen to noises from the plugulator.

At first, DJ thought he had stumbled onto Radio Belfast. Then he thought he was hearing voices and had gone "schizoid"—until he realized he could adjust the volume. Finally, he came to the conclusion that he was listening to a gaggle of women who had no idea how to listen. Who spoke like he had never heard before—full speed, like an antipodean who had lived a very long time in South Africa and had smoked a ton of dope.

Then, as Wham! one and Wham! two plus the ex finally fell into a snoring slumber, DJ realized he couldn't find any on and off button; it was cheaper than he thought.

He had heard the name Pete often. *Is the great magician called Pete?* He was curious because, as far as he was concerned, no one had actually ordered an acrobatic, magician-type disappearing act, and yet he had flashed in and out and stolen the show.

Eventually DJ shouted into the dark in desperation, "Pete's not here!" and threw the whatever it was across the room; it bounced back, and then he heard a *Shhh*.

DJ realized that the plugulator was not some cheap head mic after all.

The Operators watched Wham! one, Wham! two, and DJ.

"Males behaving like rabbits," said an Operator. Others mimicked more disgusted noises, telling each other how lucky they were not to be on Earth with all its testosterone-pumping flesh and football, but they continued to watch. In fact, it was so absorbing that for a while the Operators forgot why and who they were watching.

"Have you deleted those files yet?" said the third in command.

"Err. No, not yet. We are still trying to work out how to without leaving a trace."

Truth was they got so caught up in the rocking of a caravan they hadn't had time to read the manual for demolishing without evidence.

They were all a lower caste of Operators, assigned to watch, monitor, and report to Hilda the "carry-ons" of DJ, his two Wham! counterparts and, later, Jessie with her high-pitched squeal. None of them had ever had the privilege of watching Earth before; the only thing they were allowed to watch was the incoming members of the chambers, along with any cleaners who had forgotten how to be incognito. And the only men they saw were ancient footmen staring into the distance trying not to fall over when they dozed. Watching an Identity [1]close up was something they never even heard of, let alone dreamed of, and they were much more interesting than they had been led to believe.

Hilda chose them. "I want the trainees to learn," she said to the first, second, and third in command, as well as the secretary of the Operators. They argued, knowing full well that the trainees had no idea how to remove Pete's log from the plugulator, but Hilda had control. She knew a trainee had no experience in tampering with evidence.

"What's a wanker?" said one of the younger Operators, unaware that Hilda had just breezed in to see if there were any updates.

Hilda said nothing but began to read the script printout of what the operator had been watching. "Has this been *transferred?*" she finally said. "Has anyone seen this?"

The Operators were about to say no when Hilda spotted DJ on the screen wearing the plugulator. "What the gingersnap is he doing with that on?"

"It's Pete's," said the voice from the back.

"Pete's? I know it's Pete's, but why is this . . . DJ wearing it? I thought you said you could dismantle it, dematerialize it or something?"

"It was a theory," said the voice from the back.

"Shut up," said the first Operator in command.

"Go on," said Hilda.

"It was a theory we were working on . . . sort of." The voice trailed away as others muttered "wanker" and "can it" in the background.

"Theory—what good is that to me? You said you could fix it and now the plugulator is connected to an Identity."

"As I said, nothing to worry about."

Hilda stopped. "I mean, look at him. He's curious. He'll soon be poking about, and where will that lead . . . wait a minute, what is that?"

"It's nothing," said the second in command.

"Doesn't look like nothing to me," said Hilda.

"No, seriously, it's . . . nothing."

"Nothing?"

"Yes . . . no need to worry."

"No need to worry?" said Hilda. "Worry is what I am paid to do."

Hilda stared at the image on the screen. As she zoomed in on the plugulator, she saw it—the extra storage chip. And as she zoomed closer, there it was—Pete's log, waiting to be downloaded, intercepted, used, and/or destroyed. *What are these pickled-egg idiots playing at?*

"We could access the files ourselves," piped up the voice from the back.

"Shut it," muttered a few in the back beside her.

"What, how—and why was I not told before?"

"Ma'am," said the second in command, "what of possible interest could be on a robot's log?"

"That's for me to decide."

"And then there is the personal data," said the third in command, "laws we must abide by . . ."

"Oh, that's just for the masses—we don't have to worry about that."

"And there are all the knobs and things," muttered the forth in command. The secretary joined in. "Yes, yes, you don't want to upset the balance of, err, things . . ."

"You're just making up excuses now."

"Robots have rights too," shouted a voice from the beverage porch.

Others agreed, some muttering, "Yes, yes, that's right," as others nodded, which was futile—the room was too dark to see.

Hilda did not move; she looked about at the shadows. "Are you hiding something?"

"You just press download on the side of the screen," said the voice at the back, which was swiftly followed by a cuff-about-the-ear noise, "wanker" in various tones, and a very high-pitched "ow!"

"I want a printout pronto of all that is on this Pete's log . . . now."

Hilda made for the printer, which for some reason stood by the kettle in the beverage porch. She stopped at the door. This DJ was trouble, she could smell it. She paused and looked about. "Turn on the *tracker*."

"Ma'am? That will drain the energy from the plugulator."

"Connect with the Nokia."

"But we are just about to telespray Pete and Woody to Buchanan Street—two Identities have been spotted."

"Shut Pete down, let them walk, or better still use public transport and use the energy from the Nokia for the tracker."

"But is that wise?"

"Wise is for me to know and you not to ask," said Hilda as she headed towards the door. "And get me Pete's download, or there'll be no more caffeine breaks."

"Wanker," hissed a voice in the background.

*W*hile DJ was waking up to voices that made him think he had had more than half a dozen ciders the previous evening, Woody was pressing buttons on his phone with a confused look, convinced that he had charged his phone up that morning. Pete stared ahead with a face like a jilted bride. He was trying to adjust to the crashing down of caffeine and sugar by contemplating his navel, a useless practice, as robots have no navel.

He wondered about the Operators.

The Operators liked Pete because Pete was the only person who was nice to them. When the powers that be wanted something they barked orders, when the footmen needed something they passed notes, and as for the masses, they didn't even know the Operators existed; and did anyone say thank you? Only Pete.

So they gave him the "unavailable to the masses" log-making equipment along with a "remember us when you make it" comment.

Pete stared at the pink cupcake with frosting oozing over the side. *They won't be thinking that now,* he thought, *they'll be cursing me.* "I have blackened every Thirty-Three Robot's name forever," he mumbled. "All four of us."

"My phone's died," said Woody.

"And I am alone."

"Mum will kill me."

"Completely and utterly alone."

"Better than facing my mum an hour late."

"Destitute," said Pete. He looked out the window. He stood out like a turtle on a table; like a pickled egg on a flapjack. He turned his empty cup in his hand. "Stuck here eating cake until I die."

Woody looked at Pete's long face.

"I can't go out there like this," said Pete.

Woody slid his phone into his pocket with a sigh. "Let's get you to Primark."

*D*J woke from a night of constant noise. He had heard noises he knew no name for, and now in the cold light of almost lunchtime he wanted to know more. *Who were these women who laughed and argued at the same time? And who was this Woody?* It seemed that everyone wanted to watch Woody, and yet no one wanted to "know" the Identities. *What did they have against the Identities? And what did they mean easy on the eye?*

He suspected it all had something to do with this great escape artist who he also now knew was Pete.

He looked at the two Wham! impersonators and Herself; it was Sunday and they weren't moving until the Chinese takeaway was open. DJ, however, had things to do. He lived and worked in Glasgow running his own "That's Entertainment" business. A business he had inherited from his father, hence the out-of-date, I-will-change-one-day name.

He poured a Nescafé, helped himself to some eggs from the fridge, and then, with a *"cheers for the great night"* text to his pals, left them snoring and headed back across the water to Glasgow.

*E*dinburgh Festival

*W*hile DJ was traveling across the water, Pete and Woody were making their way to Primark, an experience that left Pete moved in a variety of ways. The street was packed with people shoving and pushing, and as Pete and Woody tripped their way through cobbled streets they often had to stop. Woody even went missing and came back with a "there you are."

Pete, being a robot of action, waited in his incognito pose as recommended by the Robot Manual. Until he noticed the silver statue performer a few feet away doing what looked like an admirable take on an old-style incognito pose. *I can do that,* thought Pete. And before he knew it he had a pile of coins at his feet, several *come see my show* leaflets in his hands, and the silver statue performer waving all sorts of finger signs at him, which Pete assumed was a form of comradeship.

Pete and Woody looked like performers in the Edinburgh Festival: Pete covered in gold with a face that looked taut from plastic surgery —Earth's smoggy atmosphere had that effect on Teflon—and Woody, a dwarf with dreadlocks, a fondness for camouflage trousers, piercings, and tattoos, looking like a sidekick that probably *did something with fire* or told stories. And as they pushed their way through the crowds many stopped and stared; some even asked where their show was.

Pete passed many incognito poses, some of a higher standard than others; he also saw lots of performers—singers, magicians of all shapes and sizes, some men, and even some on their own. In fact, the abundance of men was almost overwhelming. He even passed a large see-through box with what he assumed was a robot with impressive flexibility folded up inside, with a man standing by the box collecting money.

"She's here every year," said Woody, "with a different man, always makes a packet."

Pete stared at the contortionist with her slim legs wrapped around her ears. *I can do that,* he thought as Woody dragged him on.

Pete's mood lightened; he felt inspired. There was a lot more to this Earth than he had been led to believe. For a start, no one had ever mentioned robots.

---

1. *The Scent of an Identity: women who have a "longing" or a "something is missing" feeling are more susceptible to the scent than contented women. Men are completely immune.*

Chapter Sixteen

CONTROL

**"Control your breath and all around will think you are in charge."
—Pete's log**

Hilda had fallen asleep with her head buried in the printout of Pete's log.

Hilda had climbed into her onesie, slapped on some wrinkle remover, and curled up in bed with Pete's log, only to discover that Pete's downloads were as much use as a Band-Aid in a swimming pool. They were completely indecipherable. Beryl wrote using pen and paper, which Pete had photographed and copied. And his writing was as illegible as Beryl's. It was the sort of scroll an ant would produce while searching for food with ink on its feet.

Good old-fashioned Planet Hy Man hieroglyphic handwriting was one thing, but this . . . it was ridiculous. You would think Pete was trying to hide something, but what robot would do that?

She set her H-Pad on alarm mode for Pete, Mex, and, *yes*, Woody, and ordered the H-Pad to read from the *Write Like an Egyptian* page—which it did, in a moronic tone that would put a hyperactive in a coma. Within ten minutes, Hilda had fallen asleep upright in her bed.

❄

*B*eryl stared into the dark sky with a whimsical sigh. What she would give to feel a gear stick in her hand, the throttle at her feet and, *sigh*, the view of Legless one more time, peddling in his Lycra on a stationary bike. The Milky Way on a clear night always made her nostalgic . . .

Time was running out for Beryl, and all her stalling tactics were as useful as a mirror in the dark. Planet Hy Man's energy was on its last legs. Beryl had tried many stalling techniques to give her time for a solution, such as banning cars, promoting walking, and proclaiming the ill effects of central heating on one's karma. She pushed raw diets and juicing, stating that cooking increased the aging process, while brewed coffee and tea had become illegal to the masses along with hot baths and hot swimming pools; as all caused delirium later in life.

The masses had been convinced—a woman in a white coat and glasses on the big screen could persuade even the Voted Ins—but for how long?

She took a sip of her caffeine blast, slid a marshmallow between her lips and continued to write . . .

*A*nother questionnaire today from Queen Snorter, which as usual I ripped and tossed like a salad undressed and ready for the bin. Her curtain fringe didn't even flicker.

*L*egless did warn me, "Never trust someone who has come up from the ranks and doesn't deny it," he said. "Self-education is dynamite in the wrong hands, especially the sort of hands that have never seen nail polish."

*A*nd how right he was—that woman was born suspicious and will never believe anyone until she has researched, surveyed, and undermined. And now she is sniffing out the real reason for the "waste of oxygen" search on the "waste-of-oxygen Planet Earth."

* * *

*B*eryl let out one of her long, whimsical sighs. She had run out of options: Mex was all she had . . . and, of course, Pete.

❄

*W*hile Beryl was nostalgically staring at her much-sought-after view of the Milky Way, Hilda had jolted awake in a whiplash fashion to the sound of alarm bells and two Identities sniggering.

"Oh, for Pete and Teflon sake," she shouted as pins and needles rippled down her arm.

Hilda, a master of multitasking, rubbed her neck and shouted, "Alarm off, replay on!" several times, waking most of the footmen in the corridor. When she saw the screen she nearly choked on the last of her distilled water. The Nokia had picked up two Identities a breath away from Pete.

What the spiced tofu were they doing in Operations? What were they waiting for?

Hilda's suspicious nature ran into overdrive. Frustrated, cross, and half asleep, she put two and two together and, as usual, came up with ten. She jumped out of bed and began to stride and flounce at the same time. Not easy to pull off in a onesie, but she managed it.

She marched past the footman on duty, pulled and tossed several of the wind chimes in a temper, and entered the shed.

"Where is that son of a sperm Pete? I need to speak to him, ask whose cockamamie idea it was to . . ."

The shed was empty and there, on the screen being replayed, was a video of the said two Identities loitering about the bra section in Primark—in full view—and talking about Legless like he was alive and kicking. And not one Operator had noticed it; they were all in the other room huddled around the refreshment corner.

In truth, the Operators were huddled together passing the standard one teabag per break while trying to work out if watching a pulsating backside in a caravan was something to be envied, shared with the Voted Ins, or deleted!

"Ach aye," said one and they all fell about laughing . . .

"Where the *hell* is everyone?" shouted Hilda and then pressed the "Speak Now" button and began to do something well beneath her role: talk to Pete.

"Dematerialization begins once I can find the coordinates, unless you talk about that goddamn plugulator, and if you don't, there are two Identities at three o'clock who can make your life pretty miserable."

Pete, who was in a Primark dressing room right beside the bra section, was deep-breathing. For some reason he seemed to think that this would relieve the unpleasant sensation of sweating, which he was now experiencing. He jolted to attention.

He had known this would come sooner or later, that someone would want to see his file and understand, but he did not reckon on the dreaded Hilda; he reasoned it would be one of the Operators who would finally succumb.

Pete took the only course of action he could think of, an "act of incognito" similar to the incognito position but with more head tilting involved . . . not easy when your head is fizzing like an Alka-Seltzer, which, if he was honest, he could do with right now.

Hilda shouted, and then, as Pete's head tilting became more manic, she began to flick switches, twisting knobs and making a complete mess of everything. She was entirely overwhelmed by the advance of a dashboard since her day in the shed but like most know-it-alls, she was too vain to ask for help. Instead she floundered like a bimbo in an airplane disaster movie. And the effect of Hilda interfering was like someone grabbing a telescope pointed at a set of coordinates and twirling it around like a marching girl's baton. It would take hours for the coordinates to be connected again, but no one was going to tell Hilda; despite the fact that she was dressed in a rabbit onesie complete with hood and ears.

❋

*H*ilda stood, breathing like a trapped wildcat, as the dashboard ground to a halt. Not one Operator said anything; not one footman who had stumbled to the shed to see what the "commotion" was about. What could they say?

"Ma'am," squeaked the voice from the back.

Hilda held up her hand to silence her while trying to slow her breathing down.

"Ma'am?"

The others shushed her, but the small voice obviously had more gumption than she sounded like she had.

"My Gran knows how to use a pen," she continued. "And she can read too."

This time there was the sound of more than one cuff around the ear.

Chapter Seventeen

THE CONNECTION

"A connection is only as good as the connector." —scribbled across the top of the shed door … by a very young Hilda

Pete and Woody headed to Glasgow on the bus (Woody had a day return ticket). Sitting on a bus with Radio 2 on full blast was a new experience for Pete, who acrobat-ed his way everywhere on Planet Hy Man with nothing more to listen to than the rustle of his Teflon thighs.

Pete didn't tell Woody about the dressing room episode, just as he hadn't told anyone he had come across Beryl's Manifesto or Hilda's Magna Carta. Pete knew his days were numbered. Once Her Leathership retired he would be obsolete, and his magnificent Teflon would be sought after for another purpose altogether.

Pete was protecting his interests. He knew secrets were more than just good stories to be told when you were old; they gave you power. And he, as a robot, had little chance of getting old without the power of secrets. Besides, he was fed up being seen as a decently put-together bit of Teflon; there was far more to him than that, and up till now it had only been the Operators who seemed to appreciate it.

Pete shivered. Now as the sugar was leaving his system he was heading into the cold panicky stage, and the loss of the plugulator began to play on his mind. Hilda screeching about it didn't help either;

what was he to do? He could try to connect, discreetly speak to that nice Operator in the back, maybe she could help.

He looked out the window and stared at the cars speeding by; they looked so free and interesting, and not at all like what he had been told on Planet Hy Man. He turned to Woody. "Better than the stomach-churning dematerialization and/or transportation," he muttered, attempting a bit of lighthearted banter.

Woody flashed a smile. He was starting to feel good. He was onto something, something that was definitely going to lead to somewhere. Woody had had that hunch since he came back from the bus stop; except at the bus stop, that hunch was of the horror-film, will-I-survive, am-I-going-mad" variety. Now he felt he was heading into a Terry Pratchett, possibly *Star Trek*, world of great and witty stories.

Woody was a teetotal, halfhearted Buddhist of minimum words with (up to now) a vague belief in karma. Now his karma had soared to new heights . . . all those years in the wilderness. He had been unemployed forever and had often felt like jumping off a bridge, and he may well have done if it wasn't for medication. Now perhaps he could send the medication over the bridge, because he had, by his side, this man—or whatever he was, from wherever he was from—to help. What sort of story was he going to make, and how many words would his family have to eat when this baby of a tale got out? All those years of being called "a foolhardy dreamer," of being told he was as thick as the slab of butter on Grandfather's piece, not to mention all the other insults.

When Woody heard the commotion in the dressing room, he knew his gut feeling had not let him down, and as he picked up the odd words like Identities and plugulator, he knew he had stumbled onto something and found the fantasy he had been looking for.

He took out a notebook and began to write, like he always did when he had more words than he could speak.

Pete watched Woody open his notebook; it was full of handwritten words. He smiled to himself—and because he was a robot it really was to himself—perhaps he was not so "finished." Woody had a pen and some paper and by the looks of things he could write, and Pete had total recall at his fingertips.

❄

The Operators room was in an upheaval. They were trying to restore connections while Beryl (ignorant but not blissful) stood at the back of the room asking why they were playing "elevator music" and "did anyone know anything about batteries and, if so, how long do they take to recharge on Earth?"

The Operator, while scrambling for coordinates, had realized that, thanks to Hilda, the lights had gone out and the silence button didn't work. Every sound from the shed could be heard on the plugulator and there was no way of controlling it. The Operators were forced to come up with the only solution available to them: to drown out the noise with music—*Quadraphonic Frank*—Frank Sinatra's songs played on a pipe organ. A leftover from the good old days when elevators required a small man to operate them.

While Hilda stomped out of the shed pretending that she had done nothing to the coordinates, the first in command ordered the voice from the back to search for the manual for demolishing without evidence—not an easy thing to do in a shed so dark you could not see the rim of your glasses.

The third in command slid on Frank Sinatra, or "our Frank," as the operator liked to call him. Beryl entered.

"My Way . . ." drowned out every noise going, including Beryl, who was now shouting, "You told me that recharging was not a problem on Earth."

The Operators played deaf; they hadn't the heart to tell her about Hilda playing Captain Kirk with the controls.

"Why is everything so dark in here?" Beryl yelled. "And what is she doing by the stairs?"

"Oh, it's Vegas," said the first in command, sticking her head out of the cupboard. "We think she has put a wire somewhere under the stairs . . ."

The secretary turned up the volume. "*I did it my way!*"

Beryl looked confused. "What; Vegas and her wears?"

"Vegas has planted a wire."

Beryl sucked in her breath as the Operators waited on the reaction the first in command was banking on. Everyone knew that the mention of Vegas to Beryl had her distracted, wired, and hopefully ranting for at least half an hour, followed by an exit.

"Vegas, did you say?" shouted Beryl.

"Yes, ma'am,"

"That suck-up . . . what is she up to now? She's so far up Hilda's proverbial she could clean her teeth." (A few pulled a face of disgust.) "If Hilda were to tell Vegas to lick a footman's toe," ranted Beryl, "she would—even though Vegas is too young to know what licking can do to a man."

The secretary led Beryl back to the door.

"Loyalty oozes out of that Vegas like jam out of a doughnut."

"Yes, yes, we all know about Vegas and her oozing," said the secretary, maneuvering Beryl outside.

"That flathead wants to stick her nose in everything—before filtering."

"Absolutely, ma'am."

*D*J sat on the ferry wondering what the hell was going on with whatever it was he was listening to. The voices had become muffled out by elevator music—organ music from the fifties, the sort that his father called crooning . . . .

Every now and then the music was blocked out by a woman called "Sirness" or "ma'am" reading the riot act about "cost-cutting batteries" and "how long did 'it' take, for God's sake?"

Then as her voice faded, another woman, called purely "ma'am," began shouting for the "goddamn coordinates" and the "need to set some bait."

DJ did doze off, and in his dream he played the church organ like a madman in a kilt that swung like a ship sail and on an organ so large he had to walk from one end of the keyboard to the other. His imagination, like his storytelling, had always been vivid, but his mother had never complained; in fact, she encouraged it.

DJ had visions and memories he told no one about, ever since his mother had told him *the Story*. His grandmother called his mother's story a load of balls, but then his grandmother thought *Star Trek* was about mountain climbing for celebrities.

DJ started to think about the first time his mother told him *the Story*. She went all peculiar at the time, closing the windows and pulling the blinds, warning him if he told anyone she'd more than "box his ears." DJ was only ten and had no idea what a box around the ears meant, but he was pretty sure he wouldn't like it. And when she turned the TV up so that the neighbors couldn't hear, his heart started to pound. Was this a spy story? Was his mother a secret agent?

"It was a hedge like no other," she had begun. "It was 1959, I remember it well . . ."

DJ hadn't liked the sound of this . . . he held his breath and tried to close his ears, which was impossible, as his mother was holding his hands.

"On a hot afternoon, while huddled behind a hedge, Legless caught a glimpse of a woman in an apron and fluffy slippers. As she bent over her basket of washing, Legless stared at her small behind pressed against her nylon skirt and lust filled his loins. Surprised at his lust, he decided to take action, an action which had not been spoken about for years on his planet."

The Story haunted him all through school, and for years DJ couldn't face washing baskets full of clothes, fluffy slippers, or aprons.

Finally, when he came of age and attended his first Identities meeting, he began to understand what his mother was trying to tell him. In fact, one of the favorite pastimes of those who attended the meeting was retelling how their mothers had told them *the Story*. When times were tough it always got a good laugh.

Chapter Eighteen

THE SECOND CONNECTION

"Swinging has no age limit." –an Identity, age unknown

Pete and Woody got off the bus, walked to the top of Buchanan Street, and stood by the Donald Dewar statue. Pete by now didn't look twice at such a figure; he had become accustomed to "men" everywhere and was beginning to think that looking at men wasn't as unpleasant as those on Planet Hy Man made out. In fact, he was beginning to think that the Voted In and the like could do well to visit Scotland; a roll and sausage, according to Woody, could be a pleasant experience. And as for those who drive cars—he had seen a few smiling, some even listened to music, many as young as any he had seen in the Operators' shed.

Pete enjoyed walking; it was so much more fun with a wig. He, against Woody's advice, chose a wig that was blond and hung down his back, almost as long as Woody's dreadlocks. And now Pete had completely fallen in love with the feel of long hair and used any excuse to *toss*, as he called it.

Woody and Pete stood outside the first coffee shop they came across—a café with not one cake to be seen, just empty tables and a sad-looking student staring into his phone.

"Shall we go in and wait?" said Woody, who was about to continue with a comment about the lack of tray bakes when . . .

Poof! Boom! Fizzle . . .

Pete, in mid nod, disappeared from the street and with a silent puff of smoke appeared at the window table inside the café. The student engrossed in his phone didn't notice. No one did except for the homeless man ("ol' fella," as Pete would say) camped in the doorway. Woody stared at Pete through the window; Pete shrugged with a "wasn't prepared for that one" look, followed by a "TV shampoo ad" flick of his hair.

Woody stared at his phone. Hadn't it died?

"A fiver and I'll keep my mouth shut," coughed the ol' fella with way too much phlegm to be healthy.

Woody turned his phone around. Did he press something?

"I said a tenner and I'll no' say anything."

Woody pressed a few buttons. The ol' fella let out a huge cough, Woody passed him a scrunched-up napkin from his pocket.

"Fifteen quid and your secret's safe," said the ol' fella.

"What?" said Woody.

The ol' fella with a face matching the scrunched-up napkin sniffed. "I know what I saw . . ."

"That person," Woody said—with the wig, it was hard to tell if Pete was male or female—"is merely a magician, showing off." He said refusing the return of the napkin with a wave of his hand.

The ol' fella slid the napkin into his pocket. "I know what I saw!" he muttered.

Woody sighed; Pete was still waving from the table, as incognito as a boil on the tip of a nose mid eruption. *He couldn't be any more conspicuous if he tried,* thought Woody. *Even the ol' fella in front of me, high on vodka, in the middle of a funeral could blend in better than Pete in an empty café.*

Woody pulled from his knapsack the tray bakes from the Edinburgh coffee shop wrapped for his mother and handed them to the ol' fella, with a "that will keep your trap shut" comment.

The ol' fella, unimpressed, gave the man, woman, or whatever it was sitting under the wig the finger and muttered a few unprintable words to Woody about Pete looking nothing like either a woman or a man and more like something out of a panto for those "visually impaired." Woody, impressed with his choice of words, placed a pound coin at the feet of the ol' fella, who, without even looking at it, asked for more.

Woody walked inside and sat by Pete. The table was dirty with empty coffee cups and half-eaten biscotti. Woody flicked a few crumbs away from his table and thought about the bus stop.

"There are others, aren't there?" he said to Pete. And before Pete had time to expand Woody's knowledge of extraterrestrials, the Nokia began to bleep.

"Hello?" said Pete.

Silence.

Woody played with a few buttons. "Hello," he shouted.

"I can see Woody," said one of the Operators with a soft, hopeful tone.

"Hi, Woody," continued the Operator.

Bunnie's face flashed on the Nokia screen next. "Who's that?" said Pete.

"Who are you?" said the Operator.

"Who the hell are you?" said Bunnie.

Pete and Woody stared at Bunnie's face on the phone as "Strangers in the Night" blasted out over the voices—no one could hear them.

*D*J walked off the ferry along with the rest of the passengers from Dunoon. Some he knew with a nod, some he didn't. They walked into the cold across the terminal and onto the train station, heads bent with just the clip of footsteps breaking the silence. It was, after all, a dark Sunday afternoon and DJ was engrossed in what he was hearing.

The elevator music was working its way through every song that Frank had ever sung. And as the organ blasted out "Strangers in the Night," DJ concentrated; he could hear "Woody and Identity" talk from the Operators. He found a seat as far from anyone on the train as he could and tried to decipher what he was hearing.

❄

The Operators were in a state of disbelief. Hilda had left under a cloud of commands, only to march back in again complaining about cycling helmets now setting off alarms on her H-Pad and could they do something about it, *pronto!* "Oh, and by the way," she said with a throwaway gesture, "the dashboard is playing up and may require a little tweaking."

"Tweaking—that dashboard is as knackered as Beryl's waistline," said the secretary.

The two Operators manning the dashboard were cursing the fact that on their shift "she who must interfere" had done just that and now they were supposed to not only follow Woody, Pete, and what seemed like half of the West of Scotland but undo what had been done, without knowing what had been done.

"What are we, mind readers?" said Operator one.

A few minutes later . . .

Poof! Boom! Fizzle . . .

"What the beetroot?" said Operator two.

"It wasn't me," said Operator one.

"It wasn't me either; it's that dashboard—Herself, it would appear, has set off the timer. Looks like it has moved Pete a couple of yards into a café—how productive."

"She hasn't a clue."

"Completely mashed it."

Operator two turned a few knobs while Operator one turned up the volume of the elevator music.

Fly me to the moon . . .

❄

DJ stared ahead. Who *were* these women? Then he heard Hilda's voice again, this time shouting about "a goddamn Identity" being "nothing more than a goddamn cyclist passing by."

"His helmet must have set it off," said Operator one, followed by a muffled, "so much for the tweaking!"

Operator two turned up the volume on the elevator music.

"*Come fly with me . . .*"

DJ stared out of the train window and tried to mask his expression. He was beginning to feel chills in his spine that had nothing to do with the cold. *Where do such women exist?*

DJ had toyed with the idea of telling his mother about the plugulator, but her knowledge was pretty much limited to one story.

"Speak to Archie," she said.

So DJ did and immediately regretted it. Archie, his pal—or mentor, as Archie liked to put it—had an irritating habit of quoting himself and took forever to express himself. He clogged up DJ's phone for ten minutes, calling himself "the fountain of all knowledge," which DJ knew to be a complete exaggeration.

"I'll sort this out," he finally said. "I'll speak to the others."

DJ tried to argue, tried to tell him to "keep it quiet"; the last thing he wanted was the whole of the West Connection to know. Why did he listen to his mother?

DJ remembered the first day he met Archie. Archie was telling *the Story* at a meeting and DJ, like everyone else, was engrossed.

"Mother was hanging out the washing; bending over a basket, when . . ."

It was the first time he had heard *the Story* told by someone other than his own mother. Since then, DJ had heard it from Archie's kind so many times he had lost count. He had been told *the Story* in German, Japanese, and even in an American accent. And each time the tale grabbed the attention of many because all Archie's "kind" had a way of telling a story that could captivate.

His mother called it the "gift of the gab," but then his mother always had a polite way with words.

DJ met Archie when DJ was, to quote his mother, "coming of age." DJ was coming to terms with the fact that he was not like other boys, which wasn't easy when you attended one of the toughest schools in Govan. It was his tenth birthday and he was standing by his mother watching her put the last of the candles on his birthday cake, and he was trying to help and getting nowhere.

After the third slap from his mother's hands telling him to stop interfering, DJ asked her, "Why marzipan when chocolate worked so much better?" A question similar to many that DJ asked.

His mother sighed and told him to go speak with his Uncle Archie.

"Storytelling and baking aren't talents you should brag about," said Archie to DJ, "not to the 'masses,' anyway."

DJ nodded out of politeness; after all, he had been brought up well. Archie, to emphasize his point, rolled up his sleeve to reveal a scar. DJ said nothing; he was not quite sure what to say to a grown-up with a scar. Even now, DJ still had no idea what the scar had to do with anything. But DJ did learn to "macho things up a bit," as Archie liked to put it, and he never looked back.

Occasionally, though, when he watched his mother ice her cakes, his urges took over and, in the privacy of their home, he decorated like there was no tomorrow.

Finally, thanks to the hard work of the Operators tweaking and beyond—and the first and second in command fending off the likes of Hilda, Vegas, and Beryl—the dashboard was almost restored to its former glory, and a picture came up as clear as soluble aspirin. There in front of them were Pete and Woody at a table with an ol' fella outside, pulling faces through the window while gesturing with his fingers—which the Operators knew was not a positive thing.

They began to talk about editing.

A few sighed as Woody finally caught sight of the "old git" and chased him off with a "you got all you're getting so piss off."

"Hello," shouted one of the dashboard Operators.

They watched Pete mouth *hello*, followed by a glimpse of Woody.

"It's Woody," shouted the secretary. The others looked up at the screen. A few sighed.

"He's so handsome," muttered someone.

Woody, unaware that he was being watched, brushed the crumbs from the table.

"And clean."

"He can clean my table any day."

A few chuckled until Bunnie's face filled the screen from Mex's connection.

"Who are you?" said the Operator.

"Who the hell are you?" said Bunnie.

Chapter Nineteen

GETTING THERE

Getting there is easy—staying there takes planning, luck, and more planning." —Woody to Pete (but Pete wasn't listening)

DJ got off the train at Glasgow Central and headed towards Buchanan Street. He passed the coffee shop, unaware of Pete and Woody sitting by the window and unaware that they were expecting him.

When Bunnie's face appeared on the wide screen, all hell broke loose in the shed. No one knew who Bunnie was and to be honest no one was particularly interested. But they knew that Hilda would flip, and Hilda had a habit of arriving without warning . . .

"Put her on hold," shouted the first in command.

"And keep her there," said the second.

"Hold—is that the same as tweaking?" said DBO, (Dashboard Operator One).

"Put a cloth on it," shouted the secretary, "and press the pause button."

The DBO stomped to the cupboard under the stairs. "First tweaking, now holding," she muttered as she pulled out the box of screen covers, taking her time to select what she thought would be the least appropriate—silk or fishnet.

DBO had spent all afternoon trying to work out a way to communicate with Pete and Woody, and without a break. Then, once Pete started muttering "I understand," the secretary and the like had taken over; like it was them who had done all the tweaking. It should have been her who got the thumbs-up from Woody—not them. Her who told Pete the whereabouts of the plugulator while joking about DJ's height.

Instead, she was left to deal with a full frontal of Bunnie's face—staring at her with a set of lashes that could sweep a barn. And she had yet to see a cup of tea, let alone a biscuit.

She pulled out the fishnet. Silk was too good for them.

*P*ete sat at the café waiting for his plugulator and the wearer of the plugulator to pass; he was poised, ready for action, like a cat watching his prey in the grass, except Pete was watching from behind a menu.

"That plugulator is my insurance," whispered Pete.

Woody nodded.

"My get-out-of-jail-free card . . ."

Woody looked at him.

"As long as she doesn't know what I know, I have a future."

Woody pushed the menu from Pete's face. "She?"

"Beryl, she who must be obeyed—as long as she is in the dark, all is good."

"Beryl? I thought it was Mex we should be worried about."

"Well, yes, but Beryl is worse, especially if you are an Android."

Woody looked at Pete's face as if for the first time. "You're a robot?"

"I prefer Android."

"That's still a robot."

"Yes, but 'Android' has a capital A."

Woody looked at Pete's identical, square fingers, one with a mood ring rammed tight like a napkin ring on a napkin. Why hadn't he seen it before? "So you're not a transvestite with a really bad tan?"

Pete ignored him as Woody continued on about plastic surgery and Adam's apples. "It's just with you insisting on a bra and all . . ."

Pete stared out of the window; the Operators told him *five minutes*.

"I can't believe you're a robot."

"Android."

"Maybe you should lay off the sugar," said Woody. "I mean, this Teflon . . . is it sugar-resistant?"

Pete sighed. He didn't have time to explain about the magic of Teflon. He was sober with a headache and a sickening feeling in his stomach—*maybe he missed this plugulator thief?* Pete peered into the crowd. "She said look out for a tall man. I mean, how tall is tall?"

Woody didn't answer.

And then Pete saw it—his plugulator, sitting on top of a head way above the crowd. DJ, six foot ten, was striding down the street straight for the café. Pete, without one thought for his cappuccino, jumped to attention.

Woody muttered "incognito" as he pushed Pete back into his seat —a few of the Operators sighed.

They waited until DJ came closer, striding with purpose until he passed the café and his back was to them. Then Woody gave Pete the nod and Pete dived for the door, sending a few chairs flying. DJ turned as Pete skidded on his spilt cappuccino. DJ clocked Pete and picked up his speed, striding down the street, oblivious to the crowd.

Pete followed. Nothing was getting in the way of him and his plugulator.

Chapter Twenty

THE LIMO

"The truth is out there, you just need the right set of glasses." – Beryl

Beryl was sitting on a plush purple leather seat in the back of her driverless car. She was staring at the glass partition window. It was made of smoky glass with a painted shadow of a male chauffeur to give the illusion of one being present, although Beryl had yet to work out who was fooled by such a silhouette.

It was one of Vegas's creative initiatives since her recent move to her new post at the "Arts and Stuff" [1]cooperative. Vegas, like Hilda, had been educated on the other side of the tracks. And she had, according to many, including Beryl, little knowledge of anything above a chocolate wrapper when it came to art. A fact made obvious to anyone who sat in the back of the limousine staring at the erect stick-like figure with a pumpkin for a head.

Beryl stared at the motionless head. She had been outmaneuvered yet again by Hilda and she still had no idea what the flat-faced cow knew.

She ran her palm over the armrest.

"Yeeees, marrrm," said the automated male voice.

"Tonic, ice, sparkly, and, let me see, how about something, err . . ."

"'Something err'? Does not compute."

"Just the tonic then . . . err, now."

"Marrrm?"

A trapdoor opened at the back of the front seat and an opened box slid out with Beryl's drink fizzing inside. A cocktail umbrella dropped from the top of the box into the glass followed by the "plop" of a grape on a stick, causing the marshmallow already in the drink to start bobbing like a plastic duck in the bath. Beryl went to pick up the glass when another marshmallow was plopped in, followed by another.

Beryl sighed and cursed the damnable Voted In and their collective sweet tooth. It had obviously been one of them last in the car.

Beryl lifted the glass as more marshmallows plummeted to the floor followed by a prolonged retraction of the flat escalator back into the box. The trapdoor snapped shut followed by a loud clatter.

Fluid in the trapdoor never really worked well.

She pulled out a pad and pen from her breast pocket, ran her palm across the armrest, and wondered about Legless.

Everyone thought he was dead . . .

*H*ilda had spent the morning in an ex-Operator's kitchen.

After several cuffs around the ear, the voice from the back was summoned to Hilda, who was now standing outside the Operators' shed staring at the printout of Pete's log. Hilda demanded to meet "the grandmother who could read hieroglyphic handwriting."

The voice at the back of the room, who was so insignificant that Hilda had no interest in her name, took Hilda to her grandmother's kitchen. Her grandmother had called her H2 in honor of Hilda, an honor that, up till now, H2 appreciated. The grandmother was one of the first Operators and was not surprised when Hilda barged through her kitchen door; she had been warned by someone who knew someone that H2 had been *noticed*, and for the first time in her life she was impressed with H2.

"I don't want to know your name or anything about you," snapped Hilda.

"It's Verruca."

"I said I don't want to know your—Verruca, that is disgusting."

"Well, that's what you get for having a man-father with a man-sense of humor."

Hilda looked at the old woman. She had more wrinkles than the footman. "Sense of humor, huh?"

"That's right. He laughed his way through three rowing machines, as well as a stationary—"

"I said I don't want to know anything, I just want you to read me this."

The old lady looked up at the kitchen screen door. It had slammed shut right in H2's face and she was peering through while knocking, an irritating habit at the best of times, but more so when they had the great Hilda herself present. *Although,* thought Verruca, *Hilda's short back and sides did her no favors; perhaps her hairdresser had a sense of humor too.*

"Now would be a good time," continued Hilda.

The old lady slid on her glasses and began. Hilda listened to the rich, robust voice; it was a voice like no other Hilda had heard, smooth, silky, and deliciously chocolaty. A lesser woman would have been lulled into a trance of drooling. But not Hilda, her steel-trap mind was sharply focused; even H2's incessant knocking didn't put her off track. Hilda, unasked, pulled up a seat. As Verruca read a few lines . . .

"So I am the Queen Snorter," Hilda muttered to the ex-Operator.

"It would appear so," said Verruca.

"And what do you make of this 'shag me and I'll shag you' note?"

"Well," said the old lady, "in my day—"

"What's a shag?" shouted H2 from the behind the screen door.

Both women stared at the whisper of a girl peering through the screen door.

"A shag," said Verruca, opening the door to let H2 in, "is an old-fashioned term for an old-fashioned form of egg making."

"Requiring two people," added Hilda.

"Being present during the said egg making—that is." Verruca looked at the confused face of her granddaughter and sighed. "It's a bird."

"Young ones," said Hilda, mildly impressed, and then turned back to the handwriting. "Are you sure she called me undermining? I mean, I thought I was subtle."

Verruca peered over her glasses. "Obviously not, and there is much more; even Legless has something to say about you."

"Legless," muttered Hilda. "I hardly spoke to him."

"Hmm. Well, you left an impression," she said and continued to read.

Hilda was intrigued. Pete's log was turning into more than an eye-opener. And Legless, according to Beryl, had an opinion on everything. He even used words like "cutthroat" and "Machiavellian." Hilda had no idea that a man could be so eloquent and perceptive.

"He said that about me?" she asked.

Verruca nodded and began to read from the 1960s Legless logs. Verruca was a curious woman, and at her time in life she had nothing to lose. She called it "living on borrowed time," or "being old enough to remember when men did more than peddle a stationary"; either way, she had no fear of satisfying her curiosity and decided to start at what looked like an "interesting bit."

The restructure of pay or good old-fashioned overtime seemed to have done the trick. I did warn them. As I said to the Voted Ins, "Commands are wasted on a crew who are paid a pittance. I mean, if your men can't even afford fresh wipes, let alone liquid soap, they are hardly going to jump to attention, are they?"

However, surprise, surprise, the Voted In were completely unimpressed.

"These men," I said, "talk of points to prove, and the other week they went into overdrive."

"Hard to believe, on a stationary," joked that smart-arsed, up-yourself Hilda.

*H*ilda smiled to herself. Not a bad line.

. . .

I told the Voted In that if they don't stump up for decent beverages for the men, then the implementation of energy would be buggered.

Of course, Legless had to put his twenty cents' worth in; that night he came to my room with some cockamamie story about how he could "deal with it." "You're a man," I said. "You can't deal with anything without my say-so."

"That's your answer to everything," he snapped, stomped back to his stationary, and peddled like there was no tomorrow, completely burning out my straighteners.

"Well, it's better than beer and Lycra," I shouted back, which it turns out was what they wanted after all . . .

*H*ilda remembered those years: the Voted Ins were running on empty and they had, according to many, forgotten their roots of cleaning and low pay.

*N*ow they sup their cappuccino and Moroccan spice like the princes they tired of. *Whatever happened to the women who took over—how could they forget? We got rid of men because they were ineffectual and now look at us, wearing suits and shouting "hear, hear" at everything and erecting ridiculously large phallic light fixtures.*

"Phallic?" asked H2.

"Penis shaped."

"I don't understand," said H2.

Verruca stared at H2 with disappointment. "Banana shaped," she said, "with more—how would you put . . ." She looked at Hilda.

"Presence, power; balls?"

They both laughed, as H2 made a mental note to not only keep her mouth shut but perhaps create some distance from her mentor granny; after all, was it not she who was responsible for H2's so-called education? It was hardly her fault she had never heard of such things as bananas with a "presence."

Beryl's writing talked about producing energy with male muscles and how it started. How men were made useless by egg popping and how "every man and his dog" headed for the gym and worked their butts off to pull a successful upwardly mobile woman, and it was then the potential for energy and cycling machines were linked.

"There was a time when looking at a six-pack was good for a woman's health," muttered Verruca.

H2 glared at her grandmother with a "what would she know" face.

The fastest men began to sell their legs (along with the rest of themselves) to the highest bidder; some even became personal stationary bike assistants until, that is, they grew too old.

Give the workers what they think they want and you walk away laughing; you can always tax later . . . that's what the great Manifesto said. Of course, Legless didn't agree, even when I told him the great Manifesto himself was "a man."

"Your point being?" he said. Honestly, give a man a view and it goes to his head.

And then, in mid sentence, Verruca looked up at the great Hilda. She had begun to read Beryl's take on *the Story* and it was different from what she, like everyone else on the planet, had been told.

Verruca, like everyone else, had been educated on *the Story*, which, in the end, tells of a burnt-out Legless with balls down to his shins, eyes as glazed as a jelly tart, and his seeds spent, lost, and limp like a used tissue. A Legless who had just enough life left in him to stumble to a dark cave in the highlands of Scotland and take the never-wake-up pill.

And as for Identities, everyone knew that was just a myth, a fairy story to tell children, as believable as the elves that live in the hedges. (Everyone but the Voted In, the Operators, and the footmen, who kept their views to themselves for the rare privilege of drinking adulterated coffee.)

But what she was reading said differently. It said not only that Legless was alive, but that he had invented the spark plug . . .

She looked at Hilda. Should she tell her?

And should she tell the rest of her clan that perhaps elves may exist after all?

----

1. *Anything gift-wrapped.*

Chapter Twenty-One

JIMMIE'S ARABIC TEA SHOP

"A cup of tea is only as good as its saucer." —Jimmie's Arabic Tea Shop, back of the menu

DJ was heading for the Sunday meeting at Jimmie's Arabic Tea Shop. It was in the West End, a place Woody knew like the back of his notepad, but, unlike his notepad, Woody had no idea of what was coming next.

Jimmie's Arabic Tea Shop was an old storehouse overlooking a derelict slope. It was very *arty*, with retro crockery and mismatched tables and chairs. *Just like Granny used to have.* It served homemade hummus, flatbreads, and olives, along with fifty types of *world teas*, by students with no sense of time. But no one cared about waiting; it was part of the charm of Jimmie's Tea Shop, along with the prayer flags blowing under the veranda and the homemade cakes that collapsed as soon as you looked at them.

And it was the perfect place for someone extraordinary and half human to blend in.

DJ pulled out his phone. "I am being followed," he said.

"Yes, isn't that the idea?"

"But I got this thing on my head . . . do you think it's a good idea?"

"Is she good-looking?"

"If you call a bright orange transvestite good-looking, well, yes."

"Sounds innocent. We haven't had a transvestite for a while, and it does rile the old boys . . . does she look like a dancer?"

DJ looked behind him; Pete was strolling across the pavement on nimble legs with a rhythmic hip roll.

"Probably." DJ paused. "And she is not alone."

"Another dancer?"

"I have no idea, but he is very short and looks like something from a circus."

"Argh—one of us then."

*H*ilda was still sitting in the kitchen with H2's granny; they had degenerated into reminiscing about the good ol' days. In fact, so engrossed were they in the banter that they didn't hear the slam of the wire door as H2 left, nor the crunch of gravel as she stomped up the path dragging her 49cc moped hand-me-down along with her.

H2 drove down the dirt track road on her 49cc peddle-start moped designed purely for Operators. Nothing like the limo, four-lane freeway experiences for the Voted Ins but far better than the dusty footpath for the masses. After all, an Operator could be called in at a moment's notice and would need to get to the shed in the nick of time, as many Voted Ins put it, which was not easy when the dirt track road was full of potholes.

H2 was not the first who, at the high speed of thirty-five miles *downhill with the wind behind her*, hit a pothole, landed on her face, and carried on, all in the name of . . . *getting there in the nick of time.*

Of course, any requests for pothole-filling were always denied, usually with the threat of cutbacks along with a confusing spreadsheet, and if this didn't do the trick, then a quick *"Do you want to go back to transportation on your feet along with the masses?"* always worked. No one wanted to join the masses.

H2 was fed up. Helping Hilda would have to have been the stupidest decision she had ever made. Hilda showed no interest in her name and would probably not even remember her face. But the Operators would, and they would never forgive her. She would be forever stuck in the back of the shed with no chance of the cheesy bit of the pizza and no rest from the tea run.

H2 parked her moped outside the shed and noted that pizza had been ordered, probably consumed. She went inside.

Chapter Twenty-Two

THE CAT OUT OF THE BAG

"A cat can meow, a cat can purr, a cat can also stick up its fur."
—Identity unknown

Beryl was listening to *Chill with the Stars* on the radio when she arrived home; it always helped her forget. She closed her eyes and took a sip of fizzy when the voice of Deidre, a young upstart of a reporter, interrupted with an annoying urgency that had Beryl regretting her choice.

"Updates from the esteemed supporter of the Esteemed; Hilda is here with the latest of the latest. Hello there, Hilda. I must say, you're looking rather Spartan tonight."

"Thank you," said Hilda.

"Miss your beauty sleep?"

"Turn it up," snapped Beryl to the volume control. Nothing happened; she sighed. "Please."

"Ma'am . . ."

"Is there a reason for the late-night conference? Anything to do with the rumored leaks?" asked Deidre.

"It is hardly my place to say," said Hilda.

"Is it true that the financial committee are aware of this over-spending?"

"This is more a question for the committee . . ." Hilda stopped.

"Are they aware?"

"It is not strictly a case of awareness but more a case of reading between the lines . . ." Hilda again paused.

"Are they aware?"

"*Aware* is such a crude word," Hilda's voice purred.

"Yes, but are they?"

"The funding committee have consolidated a proposal of balance for the said . . . missing funds . . ." Hilda's voice trailed off.

"Get me a coffee," snapped Beryl to the coffee maker.

"Did you say missing?" asked Deidre.

"Did I?"

Beryl noted the coyness in Hilda's voice. "Make it a double."

Silence.

"Oh, for the love of cucumber; since when do machines want manners?"

"Ma'am can always pour herself."

"Please!"

"Did you say missing?" continued Deidre.

"I meant untraceable," said Hilda.

"Is that not the same as missing—so-called untraceable?"

"Not in its interlaying process." Hilda let out a dramatic sigh. "As Beryl our esteemed leader has pointed out."

Beryl spluttered the rest of her fizzy. *In the name of beetroot.*

"Who?" asked Deirdre.

"Our esteemed leader," purred Hilda.

"Oh," muttered Deirdre. "Her."

Beryl listened as Hilda made her sound like a fool, like it was Beryl's indecision that caused the whole financial issue that *didn't really exist.* She listened as Hilda hinted at the missing unmentionable (Legless) with not one mention of his name. Hilda was questioning the truth about Legless, alluding to the fact that he was still "alive and kicking it up down below." She treaded a fine line of words and she did it perfectly and Beryl came out looking as bad as week-old eggs sitting in the sun.

Beryl gazed out into the gray night with the occasional flickering of lights. She opened the window and let the cool air blow in. All around the planet, millions of women were at home sleeping, living, because of her. And were they grateful? Did they even know or care who kept this planet alive and turning?

She stared at the Milky Way swirling along the horizon. *Is it all worth it, the constant fight to keep on top?*

*B*eryl looked at her H-Pad; it was flashing.

"Sir, I have Mex's coordinates for you."

Chapter Twenty-Three

THE TUBE

"To crush a man takes more than a good set of thighs." —Legless

Beryl's beehive hair faded from view, leaving Mex clutching Izzie like a James Bond Blofeld, muttering, "He's alive . . . and she wants it that way."

Bunnie took the H-Pad from Mex's hand and placed it on the table as Izzie nudged her hand for a stroke.

"Was that your boss then?" said Bunnie.

"Well, yes."

"Don't think much of her hairstyle."

"Not many do."

"Don't think much of this . . . Legless for a name either. What is he, an alcoholic?"

"Not exactly." Mex stared at the photos on the wall. Beryl had finally told her the truth, and she was speechless.

"So you got to find a spark plug now? My Don, he knows all about that sort of thing, maybe he could help."

"It's not that sort of spark plug."

"And this Legless, you've got to find him too?"

Mex said nothing. She was trying to get her head around the fact that not only was Legless alive but Beryl wanted him kept that way. She wanted him not sliced, diced, and silenced but found and watched, and then for her to wait . . . for what?

"She seemed quite wistful about him," said Mex. "I've never seen her like that before."

"People change," said Bunnie.

"Why watch a man—why wait?" said Mex. "Since when has Beryl waited?"

"Maybe she has mellowed."

Left to her own devices, Mex could easily squeeze the truth out of Legless with just a few crushes of her thighs around his head, which always worked. But no, Beryl wanted a "softly, softly" approach. Since when did that work, or for that matter why would you want it to? Mex was purely a "crush and be done with it" sort of woman, and up to now she thought her mentor, Beryl, was too.

"Mellow," said Mex, "there is nothing mellow about Beryl. She may have slowed down a bit, let a few things slide, but mellow . . ."

Mex always had a mild reverence for a woman who fought off many to keep her power, a woman with a scientific, quick-witted approach to things. Who claimed to have the planet's best interests at heart.

Mex looked down at Izzie. "You'd crush him, wouldn't you?" Izzie did nothing. She was fast asleep—patted, tickled, and fed into a submissive coma.

Bunnie, not knowing what else to do, offered Mex a whisky, who downed it like it was cough syrup, and pulled a face. *My best Islay malt* thought Bunnie, she poured another for both of them and told Mex to savor it.

Mex, with no idea what savoring meant, sniffed it like a cat at its food tray only to realize it was a day old.

"That's the best you can get," said Bunnie. "Straight from Islay—men have killed for less, a mild exaggeration but needs must—and you're drinking it like it's Calpol laced with laxatives." Bunnie tossed her whisky back and poured another.

"She asked me what would seduce him to shut up," said Mex. "Am I to seduce now? Because I have no idea about that sort of malarkey." Mex tossed her whisky back. It made a warm path down to her stomach, erupting into a loud belch. Izzie looked up.

"I just crush things . . ."

Izzie barked as Bunnie refilled her glass. And Mex, still coming to terms with her now-so-called-mellow boss, pressed play on the H-Pad.

$\mathcal{P}$ete and Woody had followed DJ onto the tube and, within one stop, realized that DJ was more than ordinary. They had witnessed a connection. Pete had read about the connection in Beryl's "Legless and the Aftermath" file, but seeing it in action was far more impressive.

The carriage was empty except for a sad-looking older woman with way too much makeup on and hair piled high into a bun. DJ had hardly sat down when his eye caught the lady's and she smiled. It was nothing and yet . . . extraordinary. As the train shook and rattled through the tunnel, the carriage, for a second, fell into darkness. Woody and Pete heard a muffled "Oooo," followed by a slap and a giggle.

The lights flashed on again, revealing the elderly woman with her hair down—well shaken, grinning, and with not a wrinkle in sight—and Pete a foot from DJ, doing his incognito pose involving a one-foot-in-the-air stance and his hand inches from the plugulator.

Woody pulled him down. "Later," he whispered to Pete.

"Later," DJ whispered as the lady stood up at her stop.

Four stops later, DJ had repeated the same connection with three other women. And each time, in the dark, Pete made for his plugulator only to be caught mid incognito pose as the light flashed on again. And each time Woody pulled him down . . .

Pete's frustration was almost at the boiling point, and so was Woody's.

$\mathcal{T}$he Operators had connected Mex to Woody's Nokia, and as Mex and Bunnie watched Pete and Woody on the Tube, Mex, under the influence of a few whiskies, tried to explain to Bunnie about Identities.

"Apparently women are attracted by their scent," she said.

Bunnie pulled a face. She was never fond of aftershave—a flashback from the days when Old Spice was the rage.

"The connection is made, followed by a trancelike hallucination."

"I see."

"Yes, and as you can see here," said Mex, replaying the scene on the tube, "they tend to go for the sad ones. She probably lives alone in a cold, empty flat—lunching for one."

"Poor thing; how terrible it must be to be on your own with only *Emmerdale* to look forward to," said Bunnie.

"Yes," said Mex. "Women can be pathetic."

They watched as Pete and Woody followed DJ onto the tube train; they watched as it blacked out for seconds and the elderly woman emerged with a "tousled, just-got-out-of-bed" look, as Bunnie put it.

Mex, confused, froze the picture and looked closer. "Tousled . . . go to bed?"

"Yes, I would say that the last thing on her mind just now is *Emmerdale*."

"*Emmerdale?*" said Mex.

"Bit like *Corrie*," said Bunnie. "But with more car crashes." Bunnie smirked at her own wit.

Chapter Twenty-Four

THE MEETING

"To meet up requires more than just an address." —an Identity of great standing

That evening, rumors were flying about a rebel without a clue and Legless getting his due—Jimmie's Arabic Tea Shop was overflowing with Identities.

It was because Don had told the others of the West End connection that DJ had come across something. "Hy Man, Hilda and Beryl," he texted to many. "Does that ring a bell?"

Identities were excited and argumentative. They all had their own ideas on what DJ had and how it related to Legless. Maybe the great Legless was still alive? Maybe his prophecy of "getting his due" was coming true? Maybe the "Rebel without a clue" was him in disguise?

The problem was that there was no Identity who had actually met Legless. So no one knew just which stories were true, and if they, whoever "they" were, were actually coming for Legless or bringing him —if they were coming at all.

In the end, after heated texts along the lines of "he said, she said," it was agreed by all in the West End connection that the plugulator would flush out something, so DJ was told to wear it as obviously as possible. DJ was happy to comply; he had learned so much: that a Spice Moroccan tea "lived up to its reputation," that Frank Sinatra sung Christmas carols, and that Beryl was the leader no one listened to while Hilda was the one to be feared. This could be a step up for him, a move from being a DJ of sorts to more important things.

"This Beryl," DJ said to Don, "do you know if Legless ever talked about her except for her exceptional thighs?"

Don laughed. All women, according to Legless, had thighs of an exceptional quality, so his source said. But then Don's *source* had always been a "thigh man" and a storyteller of more imagination than substance.

*D*J got off at Kelvinbridge Tube Station and Woody and Pete followed. Woody took the lead as Pete struggled with the road crossings; he seemed to think that a thank-you wave was required if a car stopped and traffic lights were back to front.

"Green is for panic where I come from," said Pete.

Woody didn't explain; he figured that if Pete was intuitive enough not to pat him on the head (most people do at some point when you're four foot nothing), then he was smart enough to *pick things up*. Besides, following incognito was not the easiest thing to do as a dwarf, and it took all of Woody's concentration. He patiently took Pete by the arm; for once, Woody was in charge.

If Pete had a question, it was Woody he asked, and when Woody gave him the answer, Pete didn't laugh or argue, he took it as good—a new experience for Woody. He was used to being the butt of his brother's jokes and the bane of his mother's life. No one ever asked him anything except to move if he stood in front of the TV. If only they could see him now . . .

Woody and Pete followed down a lane leading to the rustic entrance of Jimmie's Arabic Tea Shop where Scottish dance music was blasting from inside. They watched as DJ eased the gate open and with a cryptic look left it ajar and entered the cluttered patio. Hanging limply from the doorway was a tatty purple curtain with gold stars painted on it. Woody and Pete entered the vanilla-scented room.

"And now let's hear one of Jimmie Shand's favorites: the two-step," said a heavily Scottish voice followed by a chord pressed on an accordion . . .

Deeeeeeeee de de de dill-de dill-de de de dill-de dill-de . . .

Before they had time to comment, to wonder who Jimmie Shand was or who would hang such a useless curtain in the middle of winter, a hand appeared from behind the folds of the curtain.

It was an old gnarled hand with yellow fingers covered in rings, and it beckoned the woman in front of them with its forefinger stiffly.

The hand was attached to the doorframe with a contractible brace; it motioned to the woman, who threw herself into a starfish pose. The hand patted her down, pulled her phone from her pocket, and tossed it like a coin across the room into a bag hanging on the wall.

Woody and Pete looked at each other as the woman let out a long, heavy moan. Woody slipped Pete his phone, and Pete faked a cough and slid the phone into his enormously filled bra and then, for added drama, mimicked the moan of the woman.

The hand motioned to Woody, who assumed the star position . . .

*B*unnie looked at the H-Pad as Woody and Pete walked onto the patio of Jimmie's Arabic Tea Shop. "I know that place," she said. "Don goes there all the time; there are so many teas to choose from I always end up with a coffee."

*T*he Operators watched as Pete entered the tea shop and were in the middle of making jokes about the star design on the curtains when the picture blacked out along with a muffled "you take it."

The next thing they knew the screen was white. Woody's mobile was now snugly slotted between the underwire of Pete's Primark bra and a scrunched-up toilet roll—a challenge for even the most advanced technical operator.

*W*oody and Pete were ushered into different doors.

Woody, clutching an itchy-looking kilt, followed behind Fin, a large round man, into a cloakroom full of men swapping kilts and moaning about how useless the entrance hand had become.

"There was a time when that hand could tell a thirty-two-inch waist from a forty; not now. Look at *this*, I could make a tent out of it."

"I could wrap *this* around my finger," another grimaced, tossing his kilt on the floor.

"Tell me about it, look at mine; the whole world and its dog will see my knickers. Twirling will be positively pornographic in *this*."

"You wear underpants, are we not meant to be incognito?"

"In commando, I keep telling you."

The men fell about laughing.

Woody faked a laugh. It wasn't easy; he was trying to wrap a larger-than-life kilt around his small waist and failing miserably. The kilt swung well below his knees. He looked up to see the men staring at him. *There was something about these men,* he thought, *something...*

The men moved closer; one poked him. Woody stopped thinking and attempted a casual stance.

"Hey, look at Tiny Tim." The others laughed; one even pulled the kilt from Woody and flicked it at him like a towel. Woody, who was now in his large cover-everything boxers, *thank God*, wasn't sure how to take this. Until Fin took the kilt off whoever was now swinging Woody's about his head and put it on.

"That'll do me." He smiled and passed his handkerchief of a kilt to Woody.

"Cheers, mate," said Woody in a deep voice—they all looked at him.

Then it hit him what was different: he could hear them but he didn't see them speak.

Just joking, he thought, making sure to keep eye contact, and they all laughed. Woody wrapped his kilt around his waist and with a blank mind waited to see what the others did next.

*P*ete followed a woman into the darkness, his feet slipping as he tried to feel his way down several flights of stone stairs. The scent of vanilla wafted up from the bottom of the stairs along with Scottish dance music and chatter from thousands of women—*no, millions,* thought Pete, talking so fast he could not understand a word. Pete's heart began to beat fast and hard. *What was he walking into? Would they work out who he was or wasn't, and if they did, would they even care?*

The woman in front pushed open a heavy velvet curtain and Pete followed into a stone basement, dimly lit with fairy lights and candles and so smoky that Pete's eyes began to water—yet another new experience.

It was a small room full of about fifty women of all ages, colors, and sizes: mothers and daughters, sisters and friends, all chatting with excitement. They looked like they were waiting for something amazing to happen. No one noticed Pete walk in.

Pete's heart seemed to summersault. He walked past the first table and tried not to stare. Beside each table was a water-smoking pipe and on each table was a cake stand full of superb-quality baking—chocolate puffs filled with cream; cupcakes with so much brightly colored icing they could hardly stand; tray bakes covered in coconut, chocolate, or toffee; and his favorite: tiny bite-size sponges oozing cream with jam dripping down the side.

Pete, however, was too tense to eat and his bra was killing him.

*O*ver the faint tinkling of a Scottish accordion, the Operators listened to Pete's heart beating as he walked into the room. They could not see the women slipping cakes into their lipsticked mouths, sucking on a water pipe and blowing thick clouds of smoke into the air. All they could see was a pile of squashed-up toilet paper, which jostled with each move.

Over the faint tinkling of a Scottish accordion, Mex and Bunnie also heard Pete's heart beating, but neither noticed. They were now several whiskies down and Mex was telling Bunnie about Beryl . . .

"She told the whole world he died," said Mex. "She put it in the national circular; we even have a National Let's Hear It for Legless Day."

"And what do you do," said Bunnie, "get legless?"

"She said that sex on Earth was hard on a man."

"Piffle—take it from one who knows."

"Who, Izzie?"

They both fell about laughing.

"She hasn't really thought this through, has she?" said Bunnie. "I mean, he is going to want to come back, interfere, takeover, maybe even get some compensation. After all, he's been down here a while . . . he'll know about that sort of thing."

"Oh, bollocks, bugger, and beetroot, he is gonna want to run the planet or at least sit on the seat," said Mex, mimicking Beryl. The H-Pad caught her eye—it was a mass of white. She looked at her empty glass. Perhaps she had overdone the whisky . . .

The woman in front of Pete took a seat and handed her jacket to an attendant walking by.

Pete had no jacket to hand in; he was wearing a dress coat, leggings, and a fine pair of boots. All of which covered his Teflon-ic robot jumpsuit, which he knew no matter how hot he felt he must not show.

Pete loved his dress coat; it was so much more fun than the boring jumpsuit. The coat had a high neck with fur, large buttons, and a big fake glass brooch that Woody told him to take off but he refused. In fact, he was even thinking of buying similar clip-on earrings, until Woody told him how stupid he would look.

Now, as he looked around at the women sprawled out on chaise lounges like Greek goddesses, he realized that Woody was right. His earrings would have stuck out like a footman in the Operators' shed. These women coordinated on a subtler level.

Pete searched the room for a place to sit, incognito. He watched the woman in front sprawl out onto a dark velvet chaise lounge, pull a smoking pipe to her lips, and begin to suck. *I could do that,* he thought and followed suit; he had never lounged before, but it looked a comfortable pastime. As casually as possible, he walked to a dark corner of the room and sat down. The chaise lounge was like a rock-hard banana and not comfortable at all, despite how it looked. He tried several lounging poses, each more uncomfortable than the last, until finally he slipped off.

"Here, suck on this, it makes it easier," said the woman next to him, handing him her water pipe. Pete got to his feet, took her pipe, and inhaled.

"And now for a wee Gay Gordons," said a male voice from somewhere. The women stopped talking with expectant looks.

"Bring on the kilts," shouted one woman.

"Ooooh, yes," shouted another.

The voice from nowhere laughed as the curtain opened from the stage and a band with DJ at the microphone appeared. He waved to the women and they waved back.

"Let's put the gay into Gordon," he shouted as the room filled with wolf whistling.

The Operators room was now full; no one was going home. Frank, *thank God,* had been switched off, the volume had been turned up, and been turned up, and a pizza with the lot had been ordered.

Chapter Twenty-Five

DANCING QUEEN WITH SPOONS

"A kilt is for dancing, spoons are for tossing, and hair is for stroking." —Identities Manual, chapter one

"We are live," said DJ, "with Hamish on the accordion, me on spoons, and Nick on drums . . ."

"We're in the house, let's make some noise!" shouted Nick, silencing the room in an instant.

"It's Scottish night," muttered one woman.

"Kilts and things," muttered another. "Not bleeding Ibiza."

"It's ceilidh time," shouted DJ, tossing his spoons into the air with a few musical clicks. "Let's start with an Autumn Leaves quick-step." Nick began a drumroll as Hector struck a chord on his accordion.

DJ couldn't hear Frank Sinatra anymore; all he heard was the occasional round of applause after a volley of spoon playing. It spurred him on to louder playing and higher tossing, which spurred Nick to drumroll like a fiend and Hamish to curse under his breath; with a dodgy back it was hard to compete. DJ wondered what they—the women he had been listening to on the plugulator—looked like and if his spoons, appropriately played, would get their curlers rattling, like the great Legless at the washing line.

Maybe he was a chip off the ol' block after all.

❄️

*T*he Identities were warming up for their kilted entrance, some with stretches and yoga poses, others lunging or lifting their leg into the air. One long lean feller was even doing a headstand, his kilt flopped over his face.

Woody tried not to stare as he listened to a barrage of thoughts about the plugulator, Dunoon, and how many women were *out there*. He was completely out of his comfort zone, which for him was sitting in a café working on a story or, worse, looking at the vacant section. He was in a scenario that no one would believe and was being treated as one of the lads—a new and delicious experience for him. *So this is what it's like,* he thought, *to be part of a gang.* He let out a loud laugh at a joke he didn't understand and then threw himself into a couple of lunges and a squat.

"Yee-haw, you're one of us," came an ESP from the Identity still in a headstand. Woody turned with a thumbs-up as thoughts of Legless began to bombard his senses.

Over the years there had been many stories of Legless's great coming—always from nowhere special. And now a plugulator had appeared from not exactly nowhere but a town next to nowhere, and the Identities were high with excitement. *Maybe this was "it."*

Although what *it* was was anyone's guess.

"So totally unexpected," ESP-ed one to another.

"I know, so out of the blue."

They talked and joked, occasionally peering around the curtain and pulling "seen anything?" gestures at DJ, who shrugged his shoulders mid spoon tossing.

Of course, no one of the West End connection had a clue about what was under their noses. They assumed that a dwarf like Woody was just that, a dwarf, with a fondness for transvestites; a dwarf so short he couldn't even reach the kilt-and-survey hander-outer at the door. And Woody blended in so well. He filled his mind with readings of Terry Pratchett to clear it of any incriminating evidence. A perfect choice, as Terry Pratchett was not a favorite with Identities, too complicated and farfetched . . .

I mean, a turtle—laughable.

And who would suspect Pete—a transvestite? Everyone knows transvestites are artists at heart and as harmless as the fatless, sugarless cakes with fatless cream served by Jimmie. No one batted an eyelid at Pete, except to find out where his fake tan came from so they could avoid it like the full-fat, full-sugar cake with full-fat cream and jam that Jimmie no longer served.

*P*ete poured his tea and glared at the plugulator thief. The stage was quite a distance and a quick escape unlikely. He looked about the dimmed room. *Where is Woody?* He sighed and sipped his tea. *The thief's going nowhere, bide your time,* he told himself and then wondered if a cake might help.

Identities entered with their kilts swinging about their behinds, showing just enough to make a woman stare and forget her chocolate; it was as seductive as a cleavage.

"It's time for a Strip the Willow," said DJ.

The women cheered and whistled as DJ began a spirited Gay Gordons.

"Let's strip that willow dry!" *Code for the men to begin to swing their kilts so high the women would forget not only chocolate but how to behave.*

Pete watched his pal enter . . .

Woody did his best to follow, but it wasn't easy; they had long legs and big steps, and he struggled to keep up. By the time they had moved on to the two-step, the men began performing high kicks, and the women squealed with delight, Woody struggled with a strained smile on his face. He had never danced in front of anyone before, not even the mirror, and here he was trying to keep up with giants who were happily showing off their underwear like a cancan dancer in a Western. Woody twirled and completed a few small soft shoe taps followed by a comic bow.

"Well done, luv."

"He's so cute."

"And the underpants—how droll."

Commando to an Identity means underpants of huge imagination.

Underpants that a woman had never seen before: magnificent, colorful, and so much more fun than the real thing. Under the dimmed lights and smoky atmosphere, the phallic characters were lit up with fairy lights, smiley faces, florescent pliable sticks, and expandable unmentionables.

Woody, thanking God for his "I'm a knob" Christmas present boxer shorts, felt safe; the gods must have smiled on him that morning. For that morning Woody was down to his last two clean underpants: "Warning, Nuclear Waste" extra-small, extra-tight Speedos, and these boxers. Thankfully, he had gone for comfort.

The women cheered Woody on, and he began to get into the swing of things, attempting a real man's cancan—making a mental note to toss out any incriminating underpants once home. The women clapped . . .

"On yer self."

"Och, the wee man."

"Higher, higher."

"Trip the light fantastic," yelled DJ, and many laughed. "The two-step, the three-step, and the five-and-a-half-step."

"The side-step, the back-step, and slide-your-leg-up-your-man-step," yelled the audience.

The Identities began to pull women from their chairs as DJ's band moved on to a Canadian barn dance. It was danced nothing like Woody remembered from the weddings he'd been to. The Identities dipped and dived, occasionally running their fingers through their partners' hair, who had become so accustomed to this that they arrived with their loose hair free of anything "stiffening."

The Identities, despite their size and age, were light on their feet and could manipulate a woman into any step, lift her off her feet, and land her safely, sometimes on their knee as they jumped to the floor in a "will you marry me?" pose. They made Scottish dancing fun and sexy and a women feel like she was sixteen again. Once an Identity placed his hands on a woman's waist, her body was his and it obeyed every move. All she had to do was look into his eyes and her body was hypnotized into a sense of wistful arousal, just ripe for a connection.

Woody pulled up a chair by Pete.

"I am not sure, but I think if we could hit the lights, I could grab it," said Pete.

Woody took a sip of Pete's Earl Grey; apparently it was that or breakfast blend. "We should dance," he said. "Everyone else is."

Pete's Teflon-ic heart skipped a beat—*Dance, me? How wonderful!* "Do you think we could do a little dipping?" he said. "Over by the band, and then I could flick across and grab . . ."

Woody looked at his partner, and he was just about to tell him that the two of them dipping was physically impossible when Pete was whisked off his feet by Fin.

Fin was an expert waltzer and, with his hand around Pete's waist, guided him. Pete twirled across the floor, so close to DJ he was almost within grabbing reach, and then was whipped away . . .

Woody could see DJ staring at Pete with a "where have I seen that face before?" look.

Woody was about to try and stop Pete, persuade him to retreat into a dark corner, when a woman grabbed him by the arm and scooted onto the floor . . . *one, two, three, four, forward and one, two, three, four, back.*

"Make this sixty-year-old nurse feel alive again," she shouted, and Woody didn't have the heart to argue. She looked into his eyes, waiting for a connection.

Woody smiled, trying to control his mind, adrenaline pumping through his veins like an electric current. *One-step, two-step . . . Terry Pratchett; three-step.*

He passed by Pete. "Tone it down," he hissed. Pete chose not to hear, but the sixty-year-old nurse overheard.

"Tone down what, darling?" she whispered. And Woody, without thinking, went for a dip. He leaned back as far as he could, giving a quick flash of his "I'm a knob" boxers.

The nurse cackled. "I have never dipped one of you before," she said. "Shall we do it again?"

Fin and Pete twirled around the dance floor like a *Strictly Come Dancing* couple. Pete was in his element and within minutes the plugulator was forgotten. Pete began to dance like there was no tomorrow; soon the Identities stopped to watch.

Pete wrapped one leg around Fin's leg, tango style, and leaned back. In fact, he leaned so far back his hair swept the floor.

The Identities clapped, some whistled; the women silently glared—clapping and whistling was what they did—not the men. Pete shimmied his chest, and then he couldn't help himself; he slid into the splits and jumped up again.

The music stopped. It was too much—even for the Identities.

"No one likes a show-off," muttered one woman.

I'd recognize those splits anywhere, DJ thought—and Woody heard it.

The drummer, sensing a change in the women's mood, went for a slower song and shouted, "Let's have a Wild Mountain Thyme."

With a suspicious look at Pete, DJ began to sing as Fin pulled Pete close to his chest with a *"This is more like it"* ESP. The other women, mid tut, turned to their partners and Pete, bewildered, wondered what he had done wrong.

Woody made to sit down but his partner pulled him up. "Where are you going? This is my favorite," she whispered.

Woody looked into her eyes and, to quote Beryl, thought on his feet: he reached for her hair and ran his fingers through it.

She sighed and closed her eyes. Woody, on his tiptoes, sang into her ear, making the most of her closed eyes, and for a moment it worked.

"Will ye go lassie..."

It worked until they were knocked by another couple; she opened her eyes and caught Woody making "we better escape soon" motions with his face to Pete.

"What the frig are you doing?" she snapped.

The Operators heard it all through Pete's breast pocket and were trying to make sense of it under the influence of a fair amount of pizza.

Pete's shimmying was too much for Woody's phone, which had been safely lodged beneath the underwire of his bra. It slid from the bra and landed on the floor, followed by a trail of toilet paper. Fin, mid twirl, stopped and stared. An Identity of heightened curiosity, he picked up the mobile and poked it.

The Operators saw two brown eyes with very hairy eyebrows glaring into the screen, followed by a tapping with a forefinger that hadn't seen a manicure in years. A few dropped their pizzas.

"Emergency close down," shouted the secretary, which of course Pete didn't hear, but the dashboard, which still needed a little tweaking, did and responded, causing the phone to not only vibrate but play Woody's latest ringtone at full volume . . .

"Shit!" said Pete.

Chapter Twenty-Six

THE EXIT

"The bra, a weapon of illusion, is best opened after a decent warm-up . . ." —Volume One: The Apparatus of a Woman by Legless

The music stopped as everyone stared at Pete trying to switch off his phone, which was on repeat and blasting through the basement.

"Thought this was a no-phone establishment?" said the sixty-year-old nurse.

"It is," muttered an Identity.

"Then what's she got in her bra, tinfoil?"

Fin offered to look but was swiftly ESP-ed back in his place by DJ, who jumped off the stage in a flash—brandishing a spoon in each hand.

DJ had his eyes on Pete from the moment he was up on the dance floor, and he knew from Pete's first backbend that Pete was the magician from Dunoon. DJ also knew that even before he had a chance to toss his spoons in a drawer his mentor would have Pete swept away like last night's sponge crumbs—hypnotized, mediated, and story-told into submission.

DJ had to act quickly or his chances of knowing more about the women on the other end of the plugulator were slimmer than an empty crisp packet. DJ grabbed Pete's arm and whispered into his ear, "We've not got much time, the ol' girl was on a promise . . ." He nodded towards the elderly woman from the Tube and began a barrage of ESP to confuse the crowd . . .

"That explains everything."

"No, it doesn't."

"Yes, it does."

"Sorry, my problem."

"No, it's her problem."

"His problem."

"No, it's their problem."

Even the Identities were confused . . .

"Sorry, what did you say—always the quiet ones?"

"Never the quiet ones."

"He's a quiet one?"

"Aye, it's a shit tan," muttered a woman inches from Pete.

The women stared as DJ's thoughts raced from one thing to another.

And when he started to ESP about chord changes in the next song, the Identities gave up, putting his outburst down to artistic temperament.

"What are you on about?" muttered one woman.

"Yes," said another, "we came here for dancing and you're spoiling it."

The two band members, sensing a crisis of some sort, took over. They had no idea what was going on, but DJ needed help and it was up to them to give it.

"Us musicians stick together," ESP-ed Hamish, who began to play "Will You Stop Yer Tickling, Jock" extra loud, while Nick threw everything he had into a drumroll. When this had little effect, Hamish thought on his feet (not something he was known for) and began his much-talked-about, almost pornographic heel kicking, surprising everyone, including DJ and the drummer. Hamish hadn't kicked his heels in years.

"Higher, Hamish, higher," shouted a few mercenary women.

Hamish looked at DJ. *"Go—my back will be done by the chorus,"* he ESP-ed as the drummer in mid drumroll gestured to the secret "let's have a fag" exit.

The exit was known only to the band, Jimmie the owner, and a voluptuous blonde from the shopping channel, who one evening smuggled a bottle of vodka in and, after "arsing it," shouted, "This Legless shit gets on my tits and more." And as no one wanted to know what the *more* was, she was spirited through the secret door.

The trio stood on the pavement outside the exit as the rain pelted down. The women's cheering echoed down the street, but no one was listening. Woody and DJ began to talk about making a run for it, both unaware where to and both thinking that it was their idea while Pete was still trying to turn off the ringtone on his phone. They were so engrossed they didn't even hear a taxi screeching around the corner like something out of an American TV cop show.

Bunnie had taken charge. Organizing illicit getaways was something she knew a thing or two about, and she thought it was time she put the jumped-up leather granny in her place . . . after all, this was her pad. She grabbed Mex's H-Pad with both hands and shouted in her best posh voice, "Get me Don's number—now!"

"Connection's made, ma'am."

"Can you get to Jimmie's Tea Shop in five?" she shouted at Don.

"Is the Pope Catholic?" he shouted back.

DJ and Woody began to argue about who was who when the taxi dramatically screeched onto the footpath, spraying both Woody and DJ with water.

"Get in," shouted the cabbie, his engine still running.

"What?"

"Get in."

"Just do what he says," shouted Bunnie from Don's phone, and no one argued.

Chapter Twenty-Seven

HILDA RULES

"Rules are meant to be broken, but only if you make them." – Manifesto the Great

Beryl was sitting in her limo, staring at the pumpkin head painted on the glass partition. She was on borrowed time, and the only solution she could think of was punching the pumpkin head for as long as it took to hurt her hand. Not that it was really a solution, more an animalistic reaction that she had seen Legless do when he thought she wasn't looking.

Beryl seethed. *What else has flathead Hilda planned, apart from calling an "impromptu meeting"?*

After hearing the radio show, Beryl plunged into a deep despair of chocolate-eating and staring at the stars. The worst had happened; Hilda, it seemed, had found out everything, hinting to all who listened that Beryl had been "economical with the truth and more than overly ambitious about the planet's energy levels." And to make things worse, Hilda began to talk of "the stationary" and how it "may take time to bring the bike back."

Beryl spent the night in the dark with the curtains closed and emerged two days later with a "no comment" stance . . . not that anyone asked.

"Once more around the block," Beryl shouted in the vain hope that some sort of solution would come to her—even though her reputation was now smashed to pieces like broken eggshells. And the limo, as if to rub it in, chose the courtyard of greatness as the only possible block to drive around—yet again. Beryl gave up arguing and instead grimaced into the dark at the statues of past leaders lit up for the masses to pay homage to with plastic flowers—hers was now covered in a veil of calico, flapping in the wind, with all the flowers removed and a "No Flowers" note nailed to the bottom.

All those years down the tubes . . .

If only she could find out who the snitch was, how they managed to snitch, and, more importantly, if there was there a duplicate you-shag-me-and-I-shag-you note—and, if so, where?

"Is there nothing secret in this pickled egg of a place anymore?" she said to the pumpkin head.

"Ma'am."

"In this place, is everything fair game?"

"Ma'am, there is nothing gamey about a pickled egg."

Beryl stared out of the limo as it drove around the back of the shed, cursing Vegas and her perverse limo driver [1]programme, when she noticed H2 sulking behind the shed on her moped—a machine completely new to Beryl.

"Stop," shouted Beryl.

The limo, not used to such a decisive command, did exactly that—screeching on the gravel like something out of a TV police drama. "What is a Hoover doing at the backside of the Operators' shed?" *Pause.* "That is a Hoover, isn't it?"

"Ma'am, Hoovers do not facilitate sitting; they are more for the pushing."

*H*2 was sitting in the back of the shed chewing on a pizza crust left for those prone to sulking. She was putting off going in.

H2 had driven into work contemplating her future. And as her scooter bumped over potholes, her anger grew. All those years of helping Gran cut her toenails, putting rollers in her hair, while telling her tales about the shed, and what the Operators got up to. For what? To be laughed at like a useless puppy doing stupid puppy tricks?

Since the radio show, Hilda and Gran had developed the sort of relationship that involved bantering and insults, all at the expense of H2. Hilda had been back several times. It hadn't taken her long to learn that reading hieroglyphics was not for the fainthearted, so she bribed Gran instead and ended up enjoying herself.

"Don't mind her, she's phallically challenged," Gran had said more than once with a glance at H2.

Hilda's responses varied from an "inability to rise to the challenge" comment to more unrepeatable suggestions that always made Gran laugh.

Her gran had been bought and paid for with a coffee machine, a cream puff, and the promise of a nonexistent reader's seat in the room with a view. And H2 was totally fed up. Working in the shed had now become unbearable; no one was speaking to her, and her chances of moving up to the dashboard were as slim as Hilda's promises.

"No one likes a snitch."

"Us comrades should stick together."

"Not crawl up the sleeve of leaders."

"That H2 has gone too far . . ."

H2 stared across the courtyard and saw Beryl's limousine circling several times. She watched it screech to a halt and Beryl, with a fair amount of tutting, eased her giant beehive out of the car.

Beryl walked toward H2 with a stare that did not avert as her hair reverted back into its pillar. It was a walk of someone whose shoes not only fitted properly but cushioned the sole, with an erect back loosely covered in silk so posh it didn't crease no matter how many times you sat on it.

H2 was impressed; Beryl had been sliced, diced, and thrown to the lions and still she walked like a leader—although she was way too old to be intimidating, unlike Hilda.

❋

"*D*o you know anything about spark plugs?" said Beryl.

H2 shook her head.

"Thought not, no one does in this quality-control haven." Beryl looked at the sky and quickly calculated from the position of the sun; she had five minutes to arrive at her meeting.

"My gran says there is still a library left with everything about everything in it."

Beryl looked hopeful.

"From fixing fan belts to bleeding the brakes, from how to ice a cupcake to how to eat without spilling, from uniforms for tall people to cleaning a fire with no mess, from—"

"I get the picture."

"But she's not telling and I'm not asking."

Beryl glanced at the pint-size Operator dressed in hand-me-downs from some past life where coordination had never been discovered. She recognized the voice, the voice from the back of the shed—always in the right place with the right answers.

"Why are you here?" said Beryl.

"No one will speak to me when I go in there." H2 pointed to the shed.

"Backed the wrong team?" said Beryl with an I-know-the-feeling sigh.

"I'll be making cups of tea until I'm as old as Gran."

"How much?" said Beryl, scanning her square nails.

"What?"

"How much? Everyone has a price."

H2 tossed her pizza crust across the gravel with impressive force. "You cannot put a price on dignity."

"How about revenge?" said Beryl.

H2 said nothing.

"You know," said Beryl. "It doesn't take much to flap a Voted In, just a faint whiff of a crisis such as turning the clocks back, a fly breaking through one of the wired office orifices, or even a footman behaving . . . oddly. Any will have them flapping like hens in a storm."

H2 sighed. *Everyone knows that.*

"Well," said Beryl. "If you can find me the head footman . . ."

"You mean the oldest."

"Well, yes. Then it is possible we could get a little even."

H2 didn't argue and was off, quicker than it took for Hilda to take Beryl's chair.

Hilda was like a woman in the know, like a child who just discovered there was no Santa Claus and was going to milk it for all it was worth. She could have sent out plans, accusations, and set the whole planet into a panic . . . but she didn't. Instead she called a meeting, giving Beryl no idea what she had planned, a move so smart even Beryl was impressed.

Beryl stood outside the room with a view—she had to time it right.

She dislodged the receptionist who, like the limo driver, was a voice-operated silhouette, although a bit more convincing, having been designed by an ex-hairdresser, and took up an incognito position behind the desk as the head footman arrived.

Beryl looked at the footman—a first for many years—and she was taken aback. His skin looked like the paper you wrapped your garbage in. And his face was pale, the sort of pale better suited to corduroy than silk. When had he gotten so grey and old-looking? When had his uniform become so tatty; it hung on his shoulders like an extra-large blanket.

Were all footmen like that?

She had stupidly assumed that the Voted In had taken care of the footmen. It was in their job description. And they were happy enough to spend a fortune on a phallic-shaped chandelier so big it took all morning to clean; surely a properly fitting uniform would have been thought of first? How wrong was she to assume. There had been budget meetings and the usual talk of the cost of coordinating silk trousers with patent leather, for what? Nothing, by the looks of things; the footmen uniforms dated back to the days of stationary energy.

She was just about to make a few "discreet" inquiries when, through the door, she could hear Hilda begin one of her boring speeches.

---

1. *The last driver retired years ago and now mans the footman's residents' reception. He never remembers any names but he does a good toasted hemp pulp.*

Chapter Twenty-Eight

WHICH WAY DID THEY GO?

"One person's exit is another's entrance." —Hilda's first speech

Don drove to Bunnie's "incognito style," as Mex suggested. That is, he took the long route, retraced halfway, and then took the short route—just in case anyone was following. Don, whose life revolved around the bookies, the Argyll, and whatever was on Sky Sports, was happy to embrace Bunnie's urgent message.

"Like old times," he said, remembering when they used to smuggle those known to the public in through the back door. And it was exactly the same back door that had seen politicians (regional), royalty (minor), and the odd game-show host. Bunnie's secret entrance had seen many faces. Not now. The porch was no longer an entrance for any *secret* visitors, more a place for plants that she liked to think were illegal.

Mex opened the door, and Don greeted her with a big smile. "Cavalry has arrived," he said, which was received with a bark from Izzie followed by a growl.

Don followed the others into Bunnie's inner sanctum, which was now, according to Bunnie, no longer an inner sanctum but more of a bus shelter—a comment ignored by all but Don, or "Donnie," as Bunnie liked to call him. He stared at his old flame and muttered something about time being kind. Bunnie laughed, stating that time had also been kind to him, and offered him a catch-up drink when all this "business" was over with.

Mex and Pete looked at each other—a catch-up drink, with a man?

Bunnie walked Don to the door, soothing his concerns, and soon he was purring about their next meeting. "You are delicious," she whispered, and Don let out a chuckle and pecked her on the cheek.

Mex coughed. "We need to press on," she shouted, and Bunnie waved Don goodbye. "I'll call you when you're needed, I promise," Bunnie said.

Mex watched. "Was that absolutely necessary?"

"Oh, definitely—never rub a cabbie up the wrong way. You never know when you need one; besides, he didn't charge me."

Pete wondered about the cabbie; he had suspicious feelings in his insides, yet another sensation completely new to him. There was something about this *Don* he couldn't quite grasp, and it wasn't his overly friendly patting on Pete's behind (as Woody suggested) or his mildly amusing stream of banter about the rain *pissing people off* . . . there was something else. He wondered if Mex sensed it, but as he broached the subject, Mex, with a flick of her wrist (another irritating habit), told him to be quiet.

"We need to reconvene in the porch," she said, and Woody, under the insistence of Pete, followed.

❋

*H*ilda's voice could be heard across the hallway and down the stairs. She was doing her most caustic imitation of Beryl yet; even the footmen were embarrassed.

"I was merely trying to point out that we have a potential disaster on the verge of imploding and *you lot*"—pause for added drama—"seem hell-bent on turning our meeting into some sort of seventies sitcom." Hilda strode about the room, waving a flyswatter to emphasize her point. She slapped the swat on the table—a few jumped. "Honestly, we get rid of all the men and then we turn into them."

"Hear, hear," muttered a few; others laughed uncomfortably as Hilda made herself comfortable in Beryl's seat . . .

"So soon?" muttered some. "Her seat's not even cold."

Beryl, unable to take much more, queued with H2, who knocked on the door and pushed the footman wearing a "do I have to" expression into the door. The footman stumbled inside. "I think Our Sirness was speaking metaphorically," he said, causing a rumble of confusion from the Voted In: *A footman speaking?*

Hilda was unmoved and began a speech about "speaking when spoken to" when the footman interrupted with a tired, flat voice. "Do you still want this to go?"

Hilda eyed him. "What?"

"The Legless information . . . to the place where you said."

"I didn't give any placement orders . . ."

"It's just that—" The footman stopped, feigning embarrassment. "I need some shoes to complete the mission."

All eyes turned to Hilda.

"Why would he have no shoes?"

"And why had she not noticed?"

"Beryl would have noticed, she noticed everything . . ."

Hilda looked around at her gaggle of Voted Ins. "Mission?"

"Ma'am, I can't deliver with no shoes."

Beryl is behind this, thought Hilda, *playing me like a pack of CDs.* Hilda, thinking on her feet, which she seemed to do daily, was on the verge of a few "discreet" inquiries when all hell broke loose. The shoeless footman began to fumble and then crashed to the ground.

H2 slipped into the room and began to shout, "Footman going down . . . footman going down," sending the Voted Ins into a frenzy of confusion.

"Mind the cushions," said one.

"And the carpet," said another.

"There's blood," shouted H2.

Hilda looked about to see who had spoken.

H2 grabbed her chance; she jumped in, ordering like a leader in the Brownies. "Tea, girls, come on, get with it—tea with sugar."

"What, tea?" said Hilda. "Who has tea at a time like this?"

At which point another footman handed Vegas a cup of tea—*luke-*

warm—and she enthusiastically tossed the tea (milk unknown) into the face of the footman, dislodging his wig and causing him to splutter.

"Call the cleaner," shouted a Voted In.

H2, with great relish, watched as another explained that as it was sundown and not sunup, all the cleaners had gone home.

Hilda shouted for someone to access the cleaners' database, but no one listened, as the footman who was now getting into the swing of things began talking gibberish with his head tossing side to side, dribbling tea—an added touch.

"Tea, as Legless would say, is for drinking, not for tossing," muttered Harry, another footman. The other footmen began to snigger as H2 called for a collection of handkerchiefs. Beryl made her move . . .

Harry, a man who in the past could muster a polish from just the tiniest bit of spit and tissue paper, rose to the occasion. He stumbled about the room collecting footmen's lace handkerchiefs until a younger, more able footman took pity on him, allowing Harry to deflate like a soufflé. Harry was of the age when fumbling a lace handkerchief was beyond him.

Beryl dashed in and made a grab for the master H-Pad (which controlled everything and didn't need recharging). She pulled the connection from the H-Pad and slid it into her breast pocket . . .

"Is that more blood?" shouted H2.

Beryl slipped her fingers into the drawer under the table and grabbed the deluxe, digitally enhanced, high-frequency, and solar-powered plugulator.

"It's on the carpet," continued H2.

Beryl slid a few pens and pads into her bag ("for old times' sake"), as well as the all-important extra-pocketed backpack. H2 threw her a "will you hurry" look as she, feeling a little desperate, continued to shout about blood and other bodily fluids. A few of the Voted In began to gag.

"Your Sirness," said Harry, clutching a few wet handkerchiefs. "Will that be all?"

"Yes," said Beryl, "and well done."

With a ceremonial twirl befitting his uniform, Harry saluted and made for a footman's exit, followed by his "team."

"That's loyalty," said Beryl.

"That's the promise of a new uniform," said H2.

"A dime a dozen on Earth," muttered Beryl.

Beryl stood behind the shed and stared at the H-Pad. She didn't have much time. She had her backpack meticulously packed by H2, a B&B leaflet updated, and her now-purple hair teased extra high for power appeal.

"Quickly," said H2, but before she had time to flick a switch, Hilda's voice boomed from the roof of the shed as she stood astride it like a superhero with a cape flapping in the wind.

"New hairdo?" she shouted.

Beryl continued to fumble with the exit button. *How the pickled egg did she get up there?*

"Let me," said Hilda, pulling her famous whip into the air. "After all, we need to send down the best, the most discreet, but of course all on a shoestring budget . . ."

Chapter Twenty-Nine

THE ESCORT

"An escort is one of many things and not always a car." –Bunnie

Bunnie, despite her facial expression, was enjoying the sudden turn in her life. For the first time in years, Bunnie missed her weekly *Corrie* and didn't even care. How could *Corrie* possibly compete with an interplanetary transvestite of appalling taste, a wise-cracking dwarf—origin unknown—and Mex's beehive-wearing aunt whose idea of swearing involved a variety of pickles?

Salads will never be the same again, thought Bunnie, who for once was blooming grateful.

She stared into her fridge with visions of entertaining and smiled to herself. *It's just like in the good old pillow-talk days—intrigue, discomfort, and cheese for thinking . . .*

DJ listened to Bunnie's bumblebee hum as she rummaged in the fridge. Was she the earthy type who liked stories and dancing? Or was she one of those women he had listened to on his plugulator? Not that he had a chance of finding out now. Pete had swiped the plugulator as soon as he could. Jimmie's back door hadn't even slammed behind them and Pete whipped the plugulator off DJ like a plaster from a cut with as much disregard of pain as a sadistic nurse. And before there was a chance to discuss an escape plan, before Don's taxi was even thought of, let alone spraying puddles, Pete had adjusted his plugulator to sit incognito in his breast pocket with microscopic earplugs pulled from somewhere secret. And then, as if to rub it in, Pete, with a smirk, adjusted the volume.

DJ scowled. There he was walking around like an astronaut from a fifties film when he could have been walking around in style.

"Give it to me," he snapped and was just about to make a grab for it when Don rolled up, splashing Pete mid smirk.

Don, sensing tension as they made their first lap of the long route to Bunnie's, made a few jokey comments about "boys will be boys despite their dress sense," rubbing both Pete and DJ the wrong way—neither thought they had anything but impeccable dress sense.

"Technology's a bastard," Don added as he began his shorter route to Bunnie's, followed by a wink in the rearview mirror directly at DJ . . . which went down like a slashed tire. Don tilted his rearview mirror and wondered if the little man could be charmed . . .

Don was, even by Identity standards, a strange man of contradictions. He was short, old, with a large bumpy nose and dark thick lips that everyone seemed to find attractive—bar DJ. Women looked at him as he sped up the road and cars pulled over to let him pass, and DJ had no idea why—were they seeing something he wasn't?

As Don sped up the motorway heading west, he overtook and cut off a coach, which slammed on the horn, overtook Don, and then, on seeing Don, slowed down and unwound his window with an "it's yourself" comment, followed by Don tapping the side of his nose. The bus driver laughed with an "I get yer" and drove off . . .

When they finally arrived at Bunnie's, DJ watched the bowlegged taxi driver limp up the path with a speed that had both Woody and him breathlessly lagging behind. And Bunnie, a woman who from the look of her inner sanctum had taste, welcomed him. She cooed at his so-called banter, laughed at his so-called jokes, and ushered him about the place with more than a playful pat on his back—even slipping *goodies* into his pocket like some aunt with her favorite nephew. And DJ knew it wasn't all for a free cab ride . . .

It seemed Don was one of those rare breeds of men that had it in them to croon a woman, on par, it seemed, with an Identity.

DJ looked around the empty inner sanctum; where was he? And why was he here? Could he leave, and if he could, did he want to?

Maybe he should have left everything to the old cronies, allowed them to question and ESP Pete into submission, collect what there was to collect. Sure, they would have taken all the credit, glory, and whatever else was available—bragged like there was no tomorrow—put their names down in the stories of greats, like the great Legless . . .

He stared at the corkboard full of female faces. He'd never hear the end of it; he would still be stuck on that small stage, doing small things, going nowhere while putting up with his mentor-bumming . . .

He fiddled with the mouse of the computer. He could be onto something big—maybe even a lead to Legless, a first for many years. What would his mentor do? One thing for sure, his mentor wouldn't be standing here like a kid ignored, waiting for something to happen.

Then he noticed the bin full of male pictures.

*P*ete, minus his dress coat, was admiring Bunnie's collection of "no trimming required" plants in her glass porch and for a moment had the blissful picture of a life without hedges, while, Woody, feeling heroic, was already taking down notes. Never before had he braved the unknown, let alone saved an Android; he felt ten feet high.

"They called me Tiny Tim," he said.

"What the gherkin is a Tiny Tim?" said Mex.

"I don't know, but we all laughed and then they started flicking kilts."

Pete lifted up the plant and wondered how much watering it took . . .

"They toss kilts about like tissue paper," said Woody. He looked at their blank faces. "I mean no one twirls a kilt about their head and lives without a hernia—they're heavier than a wet blanket."

"Brawn is not all it's cracked up to be," muttered Pete.

"Brawn is what it is," said Mex, pushing Izzie out the porch door. Izzie, having gorged on biscuits, was now, as Bunnie warned, having a repeat performance, and Mex was feeling sick from the smell. She left the door open. Izzie looked up at her and barked. "It has its place."

"'Maybe you're the rebel,' they said and fell about laughing." Woody chuckled. "Me the rebel, as if . . . then they started talking of *expecting the unexpected as expected* in the dressing room."

"What?" said Mex.

"A rebel, coming for Legless?"

"I never heard anything," said Pete.

"Or Legless is a rebel—they were very unclear," said Woody.

"That's really helpful," said Mex, pushing the dog out again.

"Well, you try deciphering ESP conversations while camouflaging the listening with Terry Pratchett quotes and dodging flying kilts." Woody looked at Mex. "See how much you can understand."

Mex said nothing as she shut the door on Izzie.

"I mean, I didn't ask to be here, I don't have to stay. I've only been helping this here robot because he-she had no one else . . ."

Izzie began to bark; Pete sighed and let her in. "ESP-ing [1,2]on our planet has been outlawed for just that reason," muttered Pete. "Blocking out an ESP takes weeks of training."

The truth was that it was the men who were nailing the ESP-ing on Planet Hy Man, so much so that women memorized the leader's last greatest speech to block any reading until things were "under control"; for a while, men ESP-ing posed a serious threat.

Mex looked at Woody, impressed that in minutes he had worked out how to block ESP-ing while dodging flying kilts; even a woman on Planet Hy Man would have struggled. With a blank face, Mex asked Woody to stay.

❄

*D*J pulled a photo from the bin. It was of an elderly man wearing a carpet-like wig on his head—who was, according to the back of his photo, looking for a woman *who loved to laugh in and out of bed*—which, with a hairdo like his, thought DJ, wouldn't be a hard thing to find.

"Anyone for cheese?" shouted Bunnie with her head still in the fridge.

DJ pulled out another photo of the same man, this time younger, with an explosion of facial hair and a smooth shiny skull—this time looking for *friendship; a listener who also liked being listened to . . .*

"One of my best," said Bunnie, who appeared from nowhere.

DJ started.

"Never a complaint."

"What? Oh? Yes . . ."

"He took escorting to a new level altogether; his stories were to die for."

"Escort?"

"Yes, now he wants to write it all down."

DJ looked questioningly at Bunnie holding a tray of cheese, biscuits, and grapes . . . it was an impressive selection, enough to tempt even a vegan.

DJ, like Woody, was in his early twenties. He was as tall as Woody was small. He had a long straight nose and red freckles. Women could never work him out because he always looked relaxed while deep in thought about something amusing. He had such long legs that he had accustomed his walk to a slow amble to allow others to keep up. DJ, as many would say, "played his cards close to his chest" and "liked his own company."

"The stories are all about women," said Bunnie, pulling the photo from him and placing it in a drawer.

Mex, Woody, and Pete walked in. Izzie had refused to stay outside, making recouping impossible, and Izzie's explosive gas clung to the air like a gas leak.

Pete, being a robot of tidiness, began to help Bunnie, and as he picked up the photos a tingling overtook him—again. He looked at Her Leathership pushing Izzie away from Bunnie's Cheese on a Tray exhibition. "Ma'am, are you feeling anything?"

"Only when she gets my fingers instead of the biscuit," said Mex.

Pete sighed. "No, ma'am, I mean your sensors—are they not picking things up . . . clues?"

Pete, ignoring Mex's waffle about a warm breath, jumped; his plugulator was making alarm noises, along with Mex's H-Pad.

*T*he Dashboard Operator had been under the stairs for hours. She was waiting to see how long it would be before anyone noticed she was gone, and when no one did, she stayed and rummaged. She pulled out boxes of old equipment and began to pull things apart, occasionally stopping to eavesdrop on the other Operators. She even managed to sneak out for a drink when the night shift dozed off, which was when she saw Hilda astride the shed roof like some caped crusader in black . . .

Years ago, Vegas, under the instruction of Hilda, had "dropped a plant" in the shape of an old-fashioned remote in the shed. Every now and then, one of the Operators picked it up with a comment along the lines of "Remember the days when you had to point and press," which would send the other Operators into hysterical giggling and praising of their new voice-operated technology.

No one suspected the remote was bugged.

When Hilda heard Beryl and H2's conversation at the back of the shed, she was ecstatic, which for Hilda meant not shouting. Hilda was listening to replays of her radio interview with Deirdre at the time when the conversation between Beryl and H2 blurted out from the remote receiver.

"The flathead won't know what hit her," laughed Beryl. "Who would suspect a footman or the likes of . . . what was your name again?"

Hilda was prepared . . .

"You must intercept Legless," shouted Hilda, "and find the spark plug recipe."

Hilda let out a manic laugh followed by a piff-puff-poof leading to a telespray of epic proportions; Beryl and H2 disappeared under a cloud of smoke . . .

Hilda landed on the ground with a thud, dusted herself off, and folded her cape into her arms.

"Always wanted to do that," she muttered and strode into the shed.

DBO leaned back against the wall and caught her breath. What had happened to Beryl? Had the mad one done away with her? And if so, who should she tell—anyone or no one?

Still holding her breath, she crept back the way she came, via the cleaner's door.

The possibility of Hilda in charge made her feel sick. The woman was loopy. Beryl was a bit frayed around the edges, but she didn't dress like a comic-strip hero or laugh like a hyena; in fact, she didn't laugh at all, which was, in light of what she just saw, probably a good sign.

DBO leaned against the stair door. She could hear Hilda coughing for attention, which was more for effect, as the shed was already in silence.

"Time for recess," Hilda shouted.

The Operators looked up, confused.

"Recess?"

"A break . . . a well-earned one." Hilda attempted a smile.

The Operators began to mutter . . .

"What? Break? What is she on about?"

"Drop everything," said Hilda, "your Christmases have finally come; leave it all and come back when we have rebooted things."

The Operators continued to mutter as confusion set in.

"Reboot? That went out with remotes and earplugs."

"Pay is suspended," said Hilda.

"What pay?"

Oh, pickled egg, thought DBO, *I know too much . . .*

---

1. The ability to communicate without speaking aloud; a form of mind reading. Outlawed on Planet Hy Man as it made bugging—a truly profitable pastime —pointless.
2. *Unlike the Contemplation of the Navel, a practice recognized by the robot-training board as an adequate way of make the passing of time productive, as well as cutting down on minding others' business.*

Chapter Thirty

ABANDONED

"A legend is only as good as its believers." –Legless

After the cryptic message from Hilda, Mex and Pete tried to console each other that Hilda was a good leader. In truth, Mex had her doubts; she, like many, had watched Hilda with a sinking heart, and she had no idea that a takeover could happen so fast.

Bunnie plonked her teapot on the table. "So she with the beehive has left the building—so to speak?"

"Yes," said Mex with a gulp of air, "presumably she is coming here." Mex, having given up trying to turn Izzie outside, was now practicing breathing through her mouth when things got too bad, as suggested by Bunnie.

"Does Beryl like cheese?" said Bunnie.

No one answered.

"I mean, there is plenty, and she might be able to give us more *gen* on this Legless fellow."

"Hope not," said Mex. "She will just interfere and get in the way like she always does . . . we usually keep her occupied with spreadsheets."

"Ma'am," said Pete, opening a window. "It is wise to prepare for the worst."

"Yes," said Mex.

"And to accommodate all foreseeable outcomes."

Mex sighed. "There is no need to continue on in that tone. We all know you have embraced a new lingo, as they say here."

"*Lingo*, ma'am, is more of an antipodean word; here it is just known as speech."

"Yes, well, just cut the speech and talk as you would if I wasn't here. I can't concentrate, what with you talking like a dictionary, Izzie gassing us out . . . and now Herself heading down here. I mean, what are we supposed to do? Search for Legless, go home, meet Herself—which I sincerely do not want to do—avoid her, beam her up? I mean, what sort of speech was that to give us—she left the planet, not sure where she's going, but Earth's a definite possibility? And what's with the out and over . . ."

"Over and out," said Pete.

"Since when do we say such a thing?"

"Quite, ma'am."

Mex flashed Pete a look as Izzie began to bark.

Hilda, accompanied by a trumpeting fanfare, had burst onto the H-Pad screen in an enlarged fashion, sporting a severe haircut and black tie. Hilda was short, sharp, but evasive rather than to the point, closing her message before any Q&A time was suggested. One of her keeping-control techniques, picked up from Beryl.

DJ all but choked on his tea; he had no idea a woman could be so . . . dominating. Were the other women he had listened to like her? He was aware of woman's rights, lesbians, transvestites, and all manner of things, but he had yet to meet a woman old enough to be his mother, dressed like a man, and at the same time seductive to the point that he couldn't think of a word to think, let alone say. How could a woman like her spin his head so? She didn't even smile, let alone laugh, and she certainly didn't look the sort who would enjoy a good story or a rousing Strip the Willow. Yet she had DJ's heart beating fast and furious, his mouth dry and speechless, and his disappointment plummeted to unknown depths when she disappeared.

"Will she be coming back?" he muttered. No one heard. He picked up the H-Pad and began pressing things. It did nothing. He shook it, rattled it, even pushed a few more buttons. Still nothing happened.

The Operators' shed cleared almost as quickly as Beryl had disappeared, and as the last Operator left clutching her free bottle of water, Vegas entered with a small H-Pad for notes.

"I'll contact Earth first—get them all confused and distressed while you find this damnable library," said Hilda, standing by the dashboard like the captain of a ship.

"Library?"

"Yes, but first, before you go, which button do I press to shut things down? I can't remember."

"Is that wise?"

"Wise is for me to spell and you to tick."

"Pardon, ma'am?"

"No time for pardon here, put some Blu Tack on the button I press and go find that library."

"Ma'am, the libraries were buried years ago . . ."

"Not according to *our gran* . . . she gave directions here on this napkin. Now, follow like there is no tomorrow and don't come back till you have your library card stamped . . . ha-ha-ha."

"Ma'am, cards are a thing of the history books."

"I was metaphorically speaking," said Hilda.

"I see," said Vegas, pulling a face. "And what about the energy situation then?"

"I will have the girls poised and ready to fuel up if necessary," said Hilda.

Vegas looked on with disbelief—girls fueled up for what? She stared at the woman she had, up until now, never questioned.

"The stationaries are greased and ready for riding," said Hilda.

"Stationaries?" said Vegas.

"Yes, along with the rowing and running machines; they are . . ." She paused and smiled to herself. "Up and running." She chuckled. "This leadership lark brings out the best in me—what?"

Vegas stared in disbelief. "Stationaries are no laughing matter, ma'am."

Hilda turned to the screen and began telling Mex about the "disappearance of our great leader . . ."

"Ma'am?" said Vegas.

Hilda put up her hand to silence her. "No time for questions," she said to Mex on the screen and pressed the button. *All the communications have shut down* flashed onto the screen in florescent blue; the dashboard then slurred into darkness.

DBO watched through the bottom gap under the door. *Oh, my cucumber—what in the pickle egg has she done?*

*M*ex took the H-Pad off DJ and flicked the battery lid open until it snapped shut, just missing her fingers. She tried again and this time it wouldn't budge—nothing happened, instilling in Mex a silent panic. She looked at Pete; he looked at her. Then, like a spider waking up, the H-Pad stretched out four limbs from some invisible orifice, jumped from Mex's hands, raced to the window, and propelled itself out into the open . . .

It cascaded down two stories into Bunnie's backyard, landing on a branch. It wrapped its limbs around the branch and swung several times, attracting the attention of a chaffinch. The bird hopped over, pecked a couple of pecks, chirped, and then, Poof! Boom! Fizzle . . .

Black smoke appeared and then evaporated, revealing a stunned chaffinch with a blackened face and a kookaburra hairstyle.

DJ made a grab for Pete's plugulator, leading to a tussle. Woody, still feeling heroic, pushed in and pulled it from them both as the plugulator lit up fluorescent blue—*emergency sign from Planet Hy Man.*

"Self-destruction begins in five . . . four . . ."

"Bollocks."

"Beetroot."

"Three . . ."

"Shit!"

Woody, without a word, raced full pelt outside; he not only thought on his feet, he moved on his feet.

"*Two . . .*"

He threw the now-smoldering plugulator in the bin.

"*Two and a half . . .*"

He slammed the lid tight, slapped a few stones on top of the lid, and raced back inside. "Get down," he shouted as garbage, after a muffled *poof*, blew into the air and fluttered back down.

"You have now been disconnected," echoed an automatic voice into the air.

*D*BO spent a few hours staring into the dark as Hilda shut down the shed and left. She flicked on her illegal H-Pad, put together roughly from an old plugulator dumped behind one of the boxes. She had with her a dynamo flashlight from an old stationary from years back when men were young and riding stationeries in the dark to save electricity. She shone her light about under the stairs; there was so much unused equipment she could be kept busy for days.

She was good at not only pulling things apart but rebuilding, remodeling, and sometimes reinventing. She had fixed H2's gran's cooker many times. She had reset her moped speed system to go uphill in first rather than be pushed; she even took off the starting pedal and replaced it with a key. She had adjusted the lighting outside the shed so at night it stayed on longer than the regulation thirty-second flash.

She was a young woman quickly learning the potential of being alone in the shed—with more out-of-date equipment than Beryl had hair colors. All she needed to do was make a few adjustments to things she had pulled apart, and then she could reconnect to the dashboard without anyone knowing. And perhaps save Planet Hy Man, maybe even go down in history as the first Operator to have a statue of herself . . .

But she needed some food, and she knew where to go. DBO slid out into the night and made her way toward H2's gran's kitchen.

❄

*B*unnie, completely fed up with no one telling her anything that made sense, decided that wine was needed to *lubricate things* and brought out the first of her coop three-for-the-price-of-two reds. Which in the end lubricated a heated discussion, leaving her as confused as Izzie's stomach was upset.

"What about this Beryl?" Bunnie said. "Will she not have the means to get you back?"

"Beryl?"

"Yes, isn't she your leader? Won't she have some sort of clout to push about?"

"Not anymore, by the looks of it; she is probably in more of a pickled-egg situation than we are, and besides, how can we find her?"

"What about this Legless then?"

"Legless? Don't think so."

"Why, is he an alcoholic? Is that why he's called Legless?"

"Legless isn't easy to find," said DJ. "No one I know has seen him. But Archie knows someone who knows someone who brought him a coffee once."

Bunnie sighed.

"He is, according to those who read minds, a storyteller of great talent," said Woody.

Mex tutted. "An action man who could ride a stationary like no other—despite his shortness of stature."

"Short? He is tall," said DJ. "The tales of his tallness are as legendary as his number of offspring. That's why he's called Legless, because he has such long legs. It's a pun; we're famous for them."

"Famous requires an audience," muttered Pete.

"He's called Legless because his legs were so short you can hardly see them," said Mex. "We have drawings of him in shorts; how he managed a stationary has always been a mystery."

"Not everything is about size," muttered Woody.

"I think you'll find he was short, so short he required a leg up to get on his stationary, and . . ." said Pete. "He drank like a fish."

"His stories were to die for and he made great chocolate that didn't put an inch on one's waist," said DJ. "Women loved him because he towered over them and made them feel safe. Of course, I am not talking of any new age storytelling of the past or a one-man comedy show. I am talking edge-of-your-seat, cliffhanger stories with"—DJ paused for drama—"chocolate . . . and he was so tall that he could, with enough run-up, hurdle a draft horse."

"I heard that Shetlands towered over him," muttered Pete.

"What's wrong with short?" said Woody.

"Absolutely, honey," said Bunnie. "Short men make a lot of things easy for a woman. Look at my best escort, he made women ecstatic . . ." She pulled out more pictures. "Just read the backs of these." Bunnie continued to rummage in her drawers and pulled out notepads and papers; a few fluttered to the floor. Pete's feeling began to haunt him again.

There's more to this man—this escort—than a need for a different haircut, he thought, and he had no idea why.

Bunnie opened a third bottle and began to pour.

Chapter Thirty-One

THE SECOND LANDING

"Fate exists only when you look back." —Bunnie

Beryl looked about; everything was black. Above her were wooden boards, beside her metal poles, and on her head dripped water. She had landed under the very scaffold Pete had landed on. But unlike Pete's landing, hers was dark, cold, and lonely; there was no audience, no music, no DJ, and no balancing on the planks. She looked about the empty street and watched as a dog trotted by and stopped to pee. Beryl was unprepared for the hot sensation spraying onto her leg. She made for a kick, skidded, and slipped straight into the puddle.

Where the pickled egg had she been telesprayed?

"Mind the dog!" shouted a man at the bottom of the street.

The dog barked and went to lick her face; she pushed him off, causing the dog to only lick more, and she was just about to pull out her whip when . . . piff-puff-poof, H2 appeared, standing in an incognito pose as practiced by the masses when those in control walked past. The dog yelled, growled, crouched, and then rolled over as H2 held her statue-like pose and would have continued doing so had it not been for her standing on Beryl's thumb.

"Apologies, ma'am," said H2 as her hand strayed to pat the dog.

Beryl rubbed her thumb. "You're here, that is all that matters."

H2 helped her up and hesitantly brushed her down. Beryl didn't argue; instead she turned to H2 to continue. "Where are we?" she muttered.

"Dunoon, love," shouted the same man who was now by their side. He looked like he had been chasing his dog for a while. He bent to catch his breath, glancing sideways at the two women. "Fancy dress?" he said.

Beryl glared at the man. He was unshaven and smelt of beer, another unfamiliar sensation.

"Aye, that's right," laughed H2, "anything for a free drink."

The dog owner laughed a "right enough," slid a lead onto his dog, and with a whistle dragged him away. The two women stared at the large man's back disappearing into the Argyll at the end of the road.

"What was all that about?" said Beryl. "Fancy dress, aye, right? Where did all that come from?"

"Just banter, ma'am. The Scots love it."

Beryl didn't say anything. BBC reruns were all the rage with certain lower-level workers, which often led to them imitating accents and mannerisms at work *until reprimanded*. Beryl made a mental note to look more deeply into such programmes—once back. She sniffed, adjusted her outfit, and tried to look about with a confident air.

"Pete landed here," she finally said.

"I know, watched it all in the shed," said H2.

"So where's the party?"

"I have no idea, but I suspect a party is not a daily occurrence."

Beryl looked at her sidekick. *Since when did she get so . . . know-it-all?* She tugged at her backpack until H2 helped her slide it off. She opened it, then remembered Hilda and cursed with every pickled veg she could think of. Hilda, along with a you-won't-be-needing-this laugh, had taken everything, leaving Beryl, for the first time in her life, with nothing but the clothes on her back and a decent hairdo.

"I've been cooked," she finally said.

"You do have your whip, ma'am."

"Yes, well, Hilda gave me that, so I have my suspicions," said Beryl. Hilda had tossed the super-light, extra-portable whip at her feet with a "knock yourself out" comment, which by the lightness of the whip and the fact that it folded into the size of a matchbox seemed highly unlikely. Beryl looked around. *So what are we to do now, apart from fight off the odd slurred comment by some passerby?*

Beryl stood out like Pete and Mex, except because she was in her eighties and in leather, the reaction was more surprised than abusive. A gran with a beehive higher than her six-inch heeled boots was a sight of great interest to all three drunks who staggered down the street.

Beryl was decked in a purple all-in-one leather jumpsuit, matching jacket, gloves, and heeled boots. The boots were designed for kicking, increasing the impact tenfold as long as, like Mex, you had good balance. Although it had been years since Beryl actually performed any kicking. In fact, she wasn't even sure if she could still do a kick without falling, but at least she was dressed for the occasion—according to Kismet.

Kismet, the official seller of all official outfits to be worn by officials and their counterparts, explained to Beryl that leather "breathed in the hot weather," *whatever that was*, and "kept you warm in the cold."

"Here we use leather to impress," she said. "On Earth it is more a case of protection."

Who was Beryl to argue? It was not like she knew any better. But now, as another taxi tooted, she was beginning to wonder.

"Are the Americans back?" shouted the ol' fella with a lusty laugh.

H2, on cue, explained that "as Americans are considered to be of a more flamboyant nature, perhaps your purple implies—joke-wise— that you are a from a time when the American Navy was based here and purple leather was seen as . . . an everyday occurrence."

Beryl glared at H2 and for the first time understood why no one wanted her about. But as she was all that Beryl had, Beryl asked if she was cold.

"Fine," shivered H2, which annoyed Beryl even more.

H2, in her neutral gray poor-man's *Star Trek* jumpsuit, looked every bit a lower-class Operator of no status. Beryl had never noticed before how poorly dressed the Operators were. H2 had no jacket, no scarf— nothing. All she had was a canvas bag packed by her loopy gran, *untouched by Hilda.*

Days ago, before Hilda's last visit and before H2 had stomped out, Gran had, as she did most days, packed H2 a small bag full of goodies along with a "just in case" comment. H2 hadn't looked because she didn't like her gran's cooking and her gran was always doing "just in case" things for H2. A solar-powered torch in case she got lost, which as she worked in a dark shed never charged up. Hot chocolate just in case the beverage corner was closed (which often happened), but once she poured it, it was noted and confiscated. And one time a watch that didn't work in a bag marked "compass," whatever that was.

Now cold, desperate, and not knowing what else to do, H2 found a large woolen jacket ("just in case you are roped into the night shift"), her flask of hot mocha drink, and an envelope with *read me when you're safe* written on the back . . .

"You going to read that?" said Beryl.

"No," said H2. "Gran is always writing notes about impending doom."

"Like now," said Beryl.

*W*hen DJ left Jimmie's Tea Shop in a flurry, Archie watched from the back door. He watched the mysterious taxi pull up with a spray of water, reminding Archie of the old days when Identities were trying to find their way, and often ended up in places dangerous and unknown. He wondered who the taxi driver was and where they were going. He decided to follow but was not prepared for Don's incognito driving.

Archie decided not to involve the old cronies as he wanted to keep DJ safe from any incrimination. Besides, whatever DJ was involved in could lead to something big. It was best to find out, see if there was anything in it for him. He ESP-ed that he was out looking for tomorrow's women and didn't wait for a reply.

He lost Don's taxi at the airport. How, he had no idea; one minute he was following the taxi around the Paisley roundabout and the next, in a flash, it was gone. Archie pulled into the next lay-by. *Where would DJ go?* Archie concentrated on his mentor—Dunoon flashed into his head, a picture of DJ's pal's caravan and the Chinese takeaway. Pleased with himself, Archie headed for Gourock and caught the boat to Dunoon—it was not often that ESP-ing stretched farther than a few miles, except when the bond was close.

"I am on my way," he said and punched the air.

Beryl pulled the envelope from H2. What an old woman from the wrong side of things would have to say of importance, she had no idea, but . . . what else could they do? She read the note to herself, her lips mouthing each word, making a whisper of a sound.

H2 watched as a group of women trotted into the Argyll dressed inappropriately for the weather and in shoes that let the rain in—just as her gran had said.

"She says, when in doubt, go to a pub." Beryl looked at H2. "What's that? And then she says to use taxis, as the drivers know everything, and always tip?" Beryl sighed. "I have heard of these taxis, but what the pickled egg is a tip?"

H2 watched as a taxi pulled up outside the Argyll and more women poured out, laughing and yelling.

"Let's follow them," said H2. "It's bound to be warmer in there than it is here, and I have this." She pulled out a purse from her jacket.

Beryl looked questioningly at H2. "I thought Hilda took everything."

H2 muttered something about how starving can clarify the brain, which had Beryl flummoxed; she had no idea what starving was.

"I saw her on the roof."

"Oh, really? Before I did, you mean?"

"Yes, I had seconds—and we Operators learn to make the most of them."

Beryl was about to mutter how grateful she was to be stuck with such a smart-arse when she realized that H2 was all she had.

She felt a little sick.

Chapter Thirty-Two

THE KITTY

"A kitty by any other name still needs feeding." —Anon, ladies' door at the Argyll Dunoon

Beryl and H2 walked into the hotel. The warm air and bright lights took them by surprise, as did the sudden silence of conversation. Everyone stared. They stuck out like spinach clinging to a front tooth.

Beryl shrugged her shoulders. "Fancy dress," she said, pleased with herself.

"Aye, right," laughed H2 with a red face as she pulled Beryl to a seat near the bar.

H2, using her best Scottish accent, ordered something "dry and white," as instructed by Gran's "how to survive anywhere" note. After repeating it three times, she gave up and went back to the "Queen's English."

Beryl threw her a "told you so look" and H2 threw her a "do any better" look back, which Beryl chose to ignore with a now-perfected shrugging of her shoulders. She followed this with an "I am the leader" chest-expansion stance, causing more people to stare than Beryl was comfortable with. H2 glared with another "told you so" look and Beryl blushed—something she had never done before. Her body heated up so quickly she was taken aback and began to fan herself with a beer mat.

"I know the feeling," said an older-looking woman walking past, and Beryl without thinking smiled back.

The hotel was full of women and at the table beside them were two, dressed like most of the others—as if there was a heat wave, which Beryl now understood the reason for. They wore their blonde hair scraped back into a tight bun, heavy eye makeup, and large earrings with lots of exposed flesh.

Beryl and H2 stared at each other, already exhausted under the strain of observing while trying to blend in. They gulped their drinks down in silence, enjoying the sensation of warmth, then ordered another. "This time with nuts," said Beryl, copying the only male standing by the bar.

"No, I'm not joking," said the first blonde, "he was doing the splits, on the scaffolding like a rubber doll."

"Magician doing the splits in Dunoon?" laughed the second blonde.

"And backbends," said the first blonde.

"Bet that DJ was pissed."

"Pissed—he was sulking big-time."

Beryl wrestled with her packet of nuts. She shook it, sniffed it, and then put it to her ear and shook it again—H2 grabbed the packet.

"You take a photo?" said the second blonde.

"Me? Oh, I'm rubbish at photos."

Two more women walked in. They were larger, with dark hair and even bigger earrings that swung down past their shoulders. They spotted the two blondes, waved, shouted, and then pulled up a seat beside them.

"Did you take a photo of the magician?" said the first blonde.

"Me?" said the first brunette, nestling into her seat. "I hate having my photo taken, it makes my head look big . . ."

"I was talking about the magician," said the first blonde.

"Has he got a big head too?" said the first brunette.

H2 tried to find opening instructions on the packet of nuts and came across "tear here," which didn't help. She shook the packet again.

"You talking about DJ? I heard he spent the rest of the night acting like he was on something," said the first brunette.

"He said he was hearing voices."

"Definitely on something, always thought he was weird . . . I mean who's his father . . . big mystery."

Beryl threw another look at H2.

The women drank fast, ordering more drinks just as fast. By the time four more women turned up, the "kitty" (not that Beryl had a clue what that was) had been filled twice and several packets of chips had been eaten but, noted Beryl, *no nuts.*

H2 looked around the room to see if anyone else had ordered nuts, hopefully with a clue as to how to open a packet. Two more women pulled up a chair at Beryl and H2's table with a "do you mind" nod, and when Beryl and H2 nodded back, the women pulled their table over to join the other women's table. Beryl, now completely fed up, pulled the packet of nuts from H2 and with her teeth tried to open the packet, sending a spray of peanuts across the two tables and the floor.

The women cackled with laughter. "Nuts, they get you into trouble every time," said one, as the barman tossed another packet Beryl's way with an "on the house" comment.

"Interesting outfit," said one woman. "Where're you from? Not from around here, dressed like that."

Beryl blushed—no one had ever called her interesting before.

"Costume party," said H2.

"Costume party? What the hell is that?" said one of the woman.

"She means fancy dress," said another woman.

"In Dunoon?"

The women's mood changed to suspicion. *I never heard of any party . . . Me neither . . .*

"Except we got it wrong," added Beryl.

"Yes," said H2. "We ended up here by mistake . . . the boss got it wrong."

The women looked at each other. "You look familiar," said the first blonde. "Have I seen you somewhere before?"

H2 jumped in. "We're with the BBC but please don't tell, it's sort of . . ."

"Incognito," said Beryl.

"Incognito," said the first blonde. "Big word. How can you be *incognito* dressed like a fetish queen?"

"That's the secret," said H2, tapping her nose and offering them a drink.

"Aye, well, I don't take too much when I'm out, just a couple of wines and then I'm on the vodka. Can't take much of the wine . . . goes to my head."

"Me neither."

"Same with me, I'm on to the vodka after this too. Too much wine will kill you."

They fell about laughing, which went completely over Beryl's head. She looked at H2. *When did she get so lippy?*

The women's conversation went from one thing to another, making Beryl and H2 giddy trying to follow. H2 and Beryl listened to many things, like how being an only child was different from coming from a large family, and imaginary friends were a thing of ridicule. That some people had cousins—which was fine but too many made Christmas *not easy*: "Imagine the potatoes." And that some women had *a man* some had *partners*, and some had other women's men or *bits on the side*. Which H2 explained to Beryl was not a side dish.

They also learned that everything was amazing after the third kitty was finished and everything was shite after the fourth. They listened as their heads got fuzzier and laughed despite not understanding. In fact, understanding just seemed to get in the way of laughing.

They learned that being a fish person had nothing to do with fishing but more to do with batter—*whatever that was*—and that fish on Earth apparently had no eyes, because as the second blonde said, "Yer cannae see under water."

They picked up on the word *piss*, a word unknown to Beryl and H2, which seemed to cause great hilarity in any context . . .

"Aye, you're talking piss, so you are."

"I'm pissed so I am . . ."

"What a load of piss . . ."

For a while Beryl and H2 forgot all about their worries until again the women talked about DJ and his secret life, which wasn't as secret as he liked to make out—despite the amount of time he spent in Glasgow on his so-called *father's business*.

"Entertainment, my arse," said one woman.

The conversation was of no help at all until one woman began to talk about Bunnie's in the West End and how she knew a friend of a friend of an *acquaintance* who had met a man thanks to Bunnie. She passed her phone around to show the Your Partner's Just Around the Corner website with Bunnie posing by her plants in the porch with a homely "you can trust me" look.

Beryl craned her neck to look. "I've heard of her," she said.

"Oh?"

"Yes, she set our friend up," said H2.

"That's right . . . err, so she did," said Beryl.

Beryl and H2 looked at the website. H2 flicked through the pages, transfixed; so many men—all ages and sizes. The only men she had seen before were the old footmen dozing on their feet.

Beryl ripped the phone from her.

"This is where we start," she whispered to H2, and H2 was just working on an affirmative reply involving the word *piss* in case anyone was listening when Archie walked in. He was looking for his pal DJ and wondered if any of the girls knew where he was.

"He's not at the caravan and I've tried the takeaway . . ." he said and stopped.

Archie caught sight of Beryl sitting regally at the corner of the table with an "I don't understand" smile. His heart stopped. The fit body of a mature woman always did that to him, especially when she looked out of place and in need of help.

"Who is that?" he whispered to the brunette, who mumbled something about the BBC and magicians.

"What's your name," he shouted across the table.

H2 looked at the advertisement on Bunnie's website, still sitting on the table, and thought on her feet—something she had learned from watching others. "Sheila," she shouted, and that funny feeling stirred in Archie's loins again.

He offered Beryl a drink and, spying nuts *everywhere*, to open her nuts if she wanted more. And before Beryl knew it, Archie was offering to take the two of them to the West End to meet the famous Bunnie . . .

"It would be a pleasure to drive such a fine woman as yourself," added Archie. And for the third time that night, Beryl blushed.

Chapter Thirty-Three

THE CLOSURE OF THE SHED

"Pretty awful or awfully pretty?" —Archie's joke for all his customers

The next morning, Hilda held a meeting with the Operators. She called them into the room with a view to impress and suppress; it had the opposite effect.

It was known to many that the room was opulent, that money had been wasted, but the Operators had no idea just how much. And, as they stared at the phallic chandelier, the plush velvet chairs, and the large panoramic view of the city, the seeds of discontent were fertilized.

Of course, keeping the Operators waiting didn't help.

They argued over whether to stand or sit while the reserve fourth in command (the least important, apart from DBO and H2) worked out that the command "now" worked on everything. And, like a child left home alone, she began to play with the curtains.

"Open—now—shut—now! Shut—open—now, no shut now . . ."

"I wouldn't do that, they look fragile," said the first in command.

"I would," said the second in command. "Those Voted Ins are living in the lap of silk, light, and space. Look at this: a coffee machine that matches the footman. What do we have? Water recycled from where— who knows—and a vent which lets in sod-all light and just as little air. In the summer we roast and in the winter we freeze."

"She's right," muttered the secretary, who hadn't spoken in years.

"Shhh, someone might be here," muttered the first in command.

"Open—now, shut—now, let's try in the middle . . . now."

The curtains stalled in the middle as a cheesy fanfare trumpeted through the room. Everyone knew what was coming next; they looked expectantly at the door.

"The Legless mission has closed down," Hilda's voice boomed from the ceiling.

The curtains sheepishly reverted to open.

"The plans for the spaceship have been discovered and destroyed and are a threat no longer."

"That's if there was a ship in the first place," muttered someone.

"But we have another emergency at hand. It seems," said Hilda, "our energy is not eternal after all but more . . . shall we say, semipermanent—like a battery. We, thanks to our esteemed leader, have a crisis looming."

The Operators began to mutter to each other . . .

"*Permanent—how can that be semi?*"

"*Running out of energy?*"

"*Is that why the shed closed?*"

"*The shed's closing?*"

The Operators began to panic . . .

"*What are we going to do?*"

"*Will the lights go out?*"

"*Lights? Who cares about the lights?*"

"*Shhh,*" said the first in command and pointed to the ceiling.

Everyone looked up to see a flap opening. Hilda's booted feet appeared on a small, round platform, followed by her black-trousered legs. The platform jutted halfway and stopped, just at the level for all to see Hilda's hands tapping impatiently on the sides of her legs. A few held their breath; the platform started, stopped, and revved into action at high speed, finally bumping onto the floor.

"Stop," said Hilda. "I said stop."

The platform continued to revve.

"You need to say *now* . . . stop—now!" said the fourth in command.

The platform grunted to a halt. Hilda adjusted her high-collared dark suit, let out an "I am in control" cough, and looked from one face to another. Everyone averted their gaze as she silently counted.

She stepped off the platform and pulled her flyswatter from her belt and counted again. A few groaned. She began to pace like a teacher looking for someone to thrash . . . tapping the side of her thigh with the flyswatter. Who was missing?

"We have plans to reinstate the stationary. Until, that is, Beryl is back from Earth"—Hilda paused for effect—"if, that is, she does come back."

The operators burst into a volley of questions.

"Beryl's on Earth?"

"Why?"

"What does she know about Earth?"

"She can't even kick!"

"What do you mean *if* she comes back?" said the secretary.

"And now that the shed is closed for rebooting, I want you to train the Voted In on how to use a stationary."

The Operators looked shocked.

"Sirness," said the second in command, "none of us know how to use a stationary."

"What's wrong with you?" said Hilda. "You can read instruction manuals, can't you?"

No one said anything.

"After all." She smirked at each Operator in turn. "I think it is time the Voted In paid their dues. These coffee machines don't come cheap, do they?"

When Hilda left the shed, DBO waited for what seemed like ages. The sun had gone down, the streetlights went on, and then she sneaked out to see H2's gran. She stopped as soon as she saw Hilda's limo outside. She crept along under the kitchen window and heard talk of a library, spark plugs, and Vegas. Her heart was set on fire; she loved spark plugs. Although she had never seen one, she had heard they were a thing of magnificence. She even had a poster in her bedroom—a drawing of a 1950s mechanic with "Sparkies plugs go the extra mile" slashed across the top.

DBO watched and waited. She saw Hilda openly parade around the kitchen, pontificating with energy. She waited until Hilda and the car had finally gone, then went inside . . .

"If you're looking for Herself, she ain't here," said Gran with a flushed face. "She's on an away day."

"If you're going to make up excuses, then at least make them decent."

"Oh," said Gran, acting all innocent, "what do you mean by that? Look, I'll show you."

She went out of the room to get her glasses and DBO filled her pockets with food. Gran's food was not the most eatable, but it was better than a limp biscuit. Gran entered with a handwritten note: *Away today, your chance to get away . . .*

Gran made DBO a flask of hot chocolate and, with a "mind how you go," saw her to the door. On her way back into the kitchen she slammed the fridge door shut, noting that finally someone had taken her synthetic soya pickled eggs . . . she had had her fill of them for a while.

*B*eryl stood bent inside the cab, struggling to pull the seat down. H2, who practically lived in the Operators' shed, had spent her life pulling things in and out of concealed cupboards, tables, beds, and desks, and like an expert she pulled down the seat and, as if it was second nature, muttered "Och, aye."

Archie looked at H2 in the rearview mirror. "How do you know Bunnie?" he said.

H2 was lost for words.

"School," said Beryl, feeling pleased with herself; she too could think not only on her feet but also propped in a seat waiting to spring back into its hole.

"That Bunnie is a woman to watch—she's not what she seems," said Archie.

And neither are you, thought H2.

Chapter Thirty-Four

THE HANGOVER

"The memory of a drunk is filled with blanks." –Bunnie

Mex woke up with the sort of head that pounded and she didn't know why. Her mouth was dry; her outfit had changed to something flowery, big, and itchy, and she didn't have any memory of how she had gotten to bed or who was making that noise in the bathroom.

"Pete," she shouted. "Pete, is that you?"

Mex slid her legs out of bed, sat up, and waited for her stomach to stop circling.

"Because if it is, you can stop it right now and tell the plugulator— *oh, bollocks; it's gone . . .*"

Pete didn't answer. He woke up with his face mashed against the armrest of a couch; his neck creaked. He lifted his head, groaned, and then put it back again. His face popped as he opened one eye and it squeaked like a new shoe. He reached into his pocket and fumbled for the plugulator . . .

"Oh, bollocks, it's gone."

He rolled onto his back and his head hit the coffee table at the end of the couch; he rubbed it as the pain radiated down the whole right side of his body. *Where the pickled egg am I?* And then he saw Woody appear from somewhere carrying two mugs with liquid spilling over the sides.

"We need to head off soon," said Woody. "Bunnie's called Don."

Pete sat up and waited for his head to catch up. *Bunnie's red wine* . . . It had been her idea to open a bottle and her idea to open another . . .

"We need some lubrication," Bunnie had said, "to lubricate—get us thinking."

Three more bottles followed, sloshing everyone into a state of heroic bonding and facilitating DJ's cornering Pete with a whisky-induced intensity that surprised Pete.

"You have the face of a listener who knows how to hold a secret," he had said.

Pete didn't get a chance to explain that all Androids were designed that way. Instead, with all escape routes blocked by a desk, a wall, and DJ himself, Pete had been forced to listen as DJ tried to unravel the mysteries of the generational gap.

"Oh, aye, we Identities have them too," he said, gesturing with a full glass of whisky. Pete watched as a few drops settled on an image of Johnny's wig.

"I mean Archie, he's a good man, but some of my friends, they just can't be bothered with him. I mean, take Nick—alls he wants to do is play at T in the Park. He has no interest in stories about Legless. In fact, he says the only interesting thing about Legless is the rumor that he once dressed as a woman to sing songs from the war—no idea which. But apparently he had the legs for heels and a voice that could reduce a newsreader to tears."

DJ sipped his whisky.

"But then, as Nick says, Archie tells a tall tale. Hamish says Nick is disrespectful and that what Archie says is true, then Nick says, 'If Legless is such a big shot, he can come and tell me himself.' Some of the lads even wonder if Legless exists at all. 'Just because we don't know who our father is and can read minds,' says Nick, 'it doesn't mean Legless actually . . .'" DJ looked at his empty cracker. "You know . . ."

Pete passed DJ the plate of cheese.

"Archie says Nick's a blowhard . . . but then Archie is a bit past it, starting to lose his mojo."

DJ slid a triangle of blue cheese into his mouth.

"There was a time," mumbled DJ, "when Archie could tell a story like no other, but not now; he's lucky if he can remember his shopping list . . ."

"I kind of like the idea of Legless," said Pete. "Where I come from, the only tool a man has is a lace hankie."

Vegas strode down the country road. At either side of her were fields of soya beans and hemp; Planet Hy Man had stopped farming animals years ago. And a woman of Vegas's thirty-odd years would not even know what a burger looked like let alone tasted like. Her diet gave her extra estrogen, extra fiber, and no bloating . . . her idea of chocolate was the dusty cocoa powder that you dipped your fingers in followed by synthetic honey or a date. Binging on food was not easy on Planet Hy Man. Usually one mouthful of anything was enough.

Vegas stared across the vast fields. In the distance, she could see the workers picking. They had no idea who she was or what she was there for—and they didn't seem to care. The rain had started and they still had half a day's work ahead of them; they were busy unfolding their rain-protection gear to put on.

Vegas, like most women of her stature, had no idea such women existed, let alone that rain-protection gear existed. She watched, fascinated, unaware of the rain dripping onto the tissue paper and washing away her instructions. Vegas, not being an outdoor woman, hadn't thought to make a copy or waterproof her instructions.

Her map evaporated before her eyes.

Vegas stared into the boggy fields. What should she do? Definitely not tell Hilda.

She decided to try the shed; if it was empty she could go back, access the backup remote—it may have recorded something.

DBO was prepared. In fact, she had never been more prepared in her life. She was waiting for Vegas to call and had practiced her answer more times than she'd clipped her granny's toenails—and her granny's toenails grew at a fast pace.

"Who are you?" said Vegas. "And why are you answering? In fact, *how* are you answering? I thought the shed was all shut down and no one could get in."

"So why did you call?" said DBO.

"I forgot and then remembered."

"I see. So what did you want?"

Vegas, now not sure what to give away, paused.

"I know more than you think I know," said DBO.

"What?"

"The cat is out of the bag."

"Are you on medication?" said Vegas.

"Take me seriously and I can help you; take the pickle and you are on your own—facing Hilda."

"Who are you?"

"DBO."

Pause.

"Dash Board Operator."

"Oh."

"And your fairy godmother . . ."

Chapter Thirty-Five

THE LEGION

"Even heroes get bunions." —H2's gran

Hilda stood outside of the shed, listening with a glass to the shed vent like she had seen people do in the movies years ago. It didn't really work, but she got the gist...

Hilda knew who the missing one was the night she stood in H2's gran's kitchen and heard the crunching of gravel around the window. Hilda, a firm believer in regular ear waxing, had the hearing of a sheep dog—finely tuned to hear what many didn't—and she decided to investigate. Hilda told the limo to drive around the corner and then she crept back and hid behind the bins put out for collection. She saw DBO enter Gran's kitchen and take enough food to feed an army of stationary cyclists.

Hilda called the youngest and rumored the smarter footman to her office. She looked at his feet. "How do you fancy a new pair of shoes?" she said. His face was unmoved. "And perhaps . . . a foot massage from my very own . . . therapist?"

Hilda smiled to herself. *If there was going to be any fairy godmother on this planet, it was going to be her, Hilda, and definitely not an Operator.*

❄

"Lace hankies?" said DJ, confused.

Pete nodded.

"I find that hard to believe."

"Where I come from," said Pete, "men, like robots, are not to be respected—it is the women who make all the rules."

"Women; can't believe that. Woman don't want to rule, do they?" said DJ.

Mex and Bunnie glared at DJ with a "what do you think" look.

He stuttered. "Archie says women are as complex as a Rubik's cube and need expert handling."

"Aye, right," said Bunnie.

"He says it can take years for a man to work out how to handle one."

"A Rubik's cube or a woman?" said Mex.

"Your Archie sounds like my Johnny," said Bunnie. "He says women are as easy to understand as a math book, but then he does make a meal out of things; I guess that's the writer in him."

Pete wanted to know more about the man with the carpet wig.

Bunnie talked of Johnny's writings—sonnets, poems, letters. "He even composed a rap," said Bunnie, "until I told him what he sounded like . . . I mean, his writings are ponderings of *them that are women.* That's about as rap-able as the Lord's Prayer."

Bunnie pulled out a box overflowing with papers and photographs of the women he had escorted. "He was so keen to please he even sent out questionnaires for escorting. 'Aren't these letters enough?' I said. 'All these photos with kisses?' 'I want to take women to another level,' he said, 'to a level they never dreamed of.'"

"This whole level issue is confusing," said Woody.

"That's what I said," said Bunnie.

Pete lifted a questionnaire and read a few comments . . .

Sweet lips, this level is completely fine by me.

He is a man who knew when to talk and when to listen, a rare breed.

Looks are not everything, darling—which according to Bunnie was just as well, for Johnny, wig or no wig, was not "easy on the eye."

"He always wanted feedback," she said, "for me to clarify and condense; speak for women. 'Why don't you use the Internet like everyone else?' I said. 'Put all your writings in a blog?' He said the Internet was bugged. So I ended up with drawers full of his stuff . . ."

Bunnie lifted up bundles of paper. A few floated to the floor as she handed them around.

"Some of these writings are straight from Legless's blue period," said Pete. "His most poignant: 'A man's vision, for all that—is just a dream,' and 'Life is like a stationary—pedaling nowhere fast.' He was a man," said Pete, "of thought—provocative, insightful, and yet, at times, incredibly . . . boring."

Pete tucked a triangle of blue cheese into his mouth and immediately regretted it. "Yes, it would appear that this Johnny has stolen Legless's work."

"Or is writing for him," said DJ.

"He could *be* Legless," muttered Woody.

"Pete, how do you know all this . . . Legless rubbish?" said Mex.

"Ma'am, it is an Android's place to know everything," said Pete.

"My Johnny's no Legless—he's just an ordinary guy who took lonely women out. Just because he's writing a boring book don't make him Legless . . . he's not someone from another planet planting his seed everywhere like some sort of . . . seed planter."

"I am one of those seeds," said DJ. "Is that such a bad thing?"

"Ma'am, the blue period of Legless is a classic expression of man's longing . . ."

"And besides," said DJ, "this Johnny is short."

"Short can be heroic," muttered Woody.

"You, an android," said Mex, "what would you know about artistic blue men and their periods?"

"This man is our key," said Woody. "And we must find him."

Bunnie, flushed with wine, pulled out her finest malt. "Good idea, Woody, Let's drink to that!"

And for Pete, everything went to a new level of *blurry* . . .

Chapter Thirty-Six

SHEILA'S DINER

"The end of the beginning or the beginning of the end?" – Pete's log

Don's car, unlike his taxi, was big and plush with a seat for everyone. Don hardly had a chance to knock on Bunnie's door and she was out ahead of everyone. She took one look, made an impressed "Oh" followed by "I'm in the front," and jumped in. She had only ever been in his taxi before.

Johnny lived across the Clyde, but as he didn't trust technology, there was no phone, no email address, just the name of a plot somewhere near Benmore Garden. A place no one had heard of but knew it involved either a trek across the Rest and Be Thankful or a ferry crossing across the Clyde.

Bunnie, in a "let's make the most of things" mood, pressed for a ferry crossing. "You'll love it," she said. "Being on a ferry is like . . . well . . . being on a ferry."

Not exactly an impressive argument, but still, without Bunnie where would they be? So no one argued; instead, they gave Bunnie the front seat and stared out of the windows at the endless cars passing by.

Don had, so it seemed to Mex and Pete, gone all out to impress Bunnie with a holiday atmosphere. He had blankets, coffee, and little bite-size biscuits to dip into the coffee and performed a running commentary of each area as they drove by.

"This place was full of shipyards; it was busier than Primark. Heaving, so it was . . ."

And if Mex or Pete knew what *heaving* was, they would have asked, "Was the place not heaving now?" But as they didn't, they watched the coastline as Don's car turned into the Gourock Ferry Terminal.

They had never seen such an expanse of grey water; the only expanse of water they saw back home were the bubbles of an extra-large bath, or the fountain of opulence in the centre of the courtyard of greatness. A fountain that spurted forth in the evenings under the stars of the Milky Way.

Don, spurred on by nostalgia, played Bunnie's favorite music, from a time when "she," to quote Don, "used to pay for her taxi fares." Not that DJ or Mex were impressed—Mex hadn't even heard of AC/DC . . .

Don bumped onto the ferry, turning up the volume on "Highway to Hell" that was pumped through Don's retro car stereo as they crossed the choppy waters of the Clyde.

"This is your favorite, Buns, remember?" said Don.

"Don't call me Buns," shouted Bunnie.

Don laughed. "That's right, Buns, they are brilliant, aren't they."

"I said don't call me Buns."

"No, you're fine, I've had plenty."

Bunnie let out a long sigh.

No one noticed the return Dunoon ferry pass the other way.

Beryl was on that return ferry. She was outside Archie's car, taking in the fresh air. She was leaning against the wall watching the waves flop against the high walls of the ferry, clutching her espresso from Sheila's Diner. Archie had insisted on taking her and H2 for a proper slap-up breakfast to brush away the morning cobwebs. He even, continuing his theme of cobweb brushing, bought a takeaway surprise: a sweet the size of a basketball called a meringue. H2 had eaten most of it, spreading as much as she ate across the back seat. Beryl escaped as quickly as she could outside while H2 cleaned up . . . sticky hands were never her thing.

The wind took her breath away . . .

Bunnie sipped her coffee. If she, as planned, had taken some fresh air, she would have looked across the Clyde to see, in the flesh, what she had seen on the now-debunked H-Pad—the pyramid hair of a Mex's pickle-swearing aunt withstanding all that the Clyde could blow at her.

Instead, Bunnie spent her time asking Don to "turn it down" and "turn the child lock off, and can you put some sugar in the coffee?" And by the time all that was accomplished, Beryl had taken her fresh air, and, clutching her empty espresso cup, returned to the taxi, oblivious to those who stared at her with a "do I know her?" look.

Beryl's walk shouted *I am worth a second look, but you'll never guess why*.

*D*on drove off the ferry and headed for Benmore Garden. They drove around the Holy Loch. It was sunny and the beauty of the hills had Mex and Pete mesmerized. Hills in their world were covered in mud and best avoided by all. Here they were lush-looking with a silky veil of mist magically suspended around the base. Mex and Pete had never seen anything like it before.

"I never thought it possible," muttered Mex.

"Me neither," muttered Pete.

"It's a hill," said Woody. "Some people climb them."

"Climb them?"

"Yes, to get to the top."

Mex and Pete looked at him.

"For the view . . ."

*B*eryl sat in the back of the taxi listening to the stilted talk from the radio and finally gave up; trying to make out what they were saying was as easy as trying to explain to a Voted In that interior design was not the be-all and end-all. They drove off the ferry and into the town of Gourock, passing shops on the ground with what looked like anyone and everyone walking into them.

In Beryl's world, the limo had tinted glass, which prevented any looking out unless you shouted "clear now" for the glass to become see-through. In Beryl's world, the planet was grey and flat and the only time one would want to look out the window of a limo was at night to view the Milky Way. Or in the early evening in the city centre to nose about who was walking where or see how many tributes lay at the bottom of the statues in the courtyard of greatness. Beryl stared outside at the shops. In her world, shops were for the elite and high up in buildings, not on the ground where the masses shuffled.

"Sheila's Diner," said Beryl, stirring the grinds of her espresso. "Anyone can go there?"

Archie threw his heroine a look in the rearview mirror. "It's a café —of course."

"I've nothing against anyone, per se, but it's a bit familiar, is it not, this 'anyone for anywhere' lark?"

"People are free to go wherever," said Archie.

"As long as they can pay," chipped in H2.

Beryl, ignoring H2, continued with her "a place for everything" speech, which H2 could mouth word for word.

"We are not home," muttered H2, "and we must remember what we are here for . . . not get sidetracked."

Archie looked from one woman to another in his rearview mirror. He had a feeling in his bunions; they always played up when things were amiss.

"So what are you really here for then?" he said.

H2 stared out at an odd-looking couple holding hands, mildly wondering if walking holding hands was at all comfortable. "You could call it digging up the past," she muttered.

*D*on drove past Sheila's Diner, where they stopped to reconvene—or, as Woody insisted, to ask for directions to this so-called address.

Mex looked at the address, Pete looked at it, Bunnie snatched it from him and looked at it, and then Don looked at it.

"Never heard of it."

Woody took the address off Don and headed to the café. His small figure strode with purpose across the car park as the others watched with an "I didn't think of that" sigh.

The café was full; there was a bus tour of elderly people, a couple of families, and several staff standing around. They all looked up and stared at the entrance as the door swung open with a creak—then, realizing it wasn't right to stare at a dwarf, turned away, only to stare at the door again as a bright orange transvestite filled the doorway—then, realizing that that too wasn't PC, turned away.

"Why is that robot orange?" shouted a small child.

"It's rude to stare and he is not a robot," snapped his mother.

"But his face is funny," said the little boy, who was now standing by Pete and looking up into his nostrils.

"I'm an android," Pete whispered to the boy.

"That's the same as a robot," shouted the boy, poking him. "He feels squishy."

"You ever seen a robot?" said Woody.

"Android," said Pete.

The little boy shook his head.

Mex, in full view of the restaurant, walked across the car park, tripped, skidded, and then, with a few pickled exclamations, tripped again. Everyone stared, and this time they didn't look away—a fifty-something half cut in the middle of the day was asking to be stared at.

Mex was not used to wearing running shoes and comfortable clothes, and she was completely unbalanced without her whip waving by her side. As she staggered to right herself, she remembered something that had been blurry since the previous night. Bunnie had taken Mex into her inner sanctum to revamp her while suggesting that the whip be placed in a safe place.

According to Bunnie, a whip in daylight was "asking for trouble."

Mex, however, could not imagine a day without her trusty friend strapped to her thigh. She knew there was an incognito button somewhere, and after several staggering attempts in Bunnie's inner sanctum, Bunnie found it. The whip collapsed like a folding umbrella. And Bunnie, impressed, amused, and pleased with herself, handed Mex her least favorite, for-the-bin handbag.

"Keep it," said Bunnie, "for your whip."

Mex stared at her carrot-sized whip. *Not as impressive or as accessible, but better than nothing,* she thought and placed it in the handbag.

Mex entered the restaurant and watched the small boy continue to poke Pete, each time a little harder.

He stared at Mex as she staggered in. The little boy's mother told him not to look; when he asked why he was told to be quiet.

By the time they had gotten to Bunnie's, Archie was beginning to wonder about the mysterious woman from the BBC; she was attractive in a Joan Rivers sort of way but suspiciously not what she seemed. She was too quick to order and looked at everything like she was seeing it for the first time. And as for H2, how annoying can one female be? Like all Identities, Archie had a fondness for women and their happiness that stretched all boundaries of age and size. But H2 pushed the limit of tolerance; she had an answer for everything, even about things he didn't know, and she didn't care who she offended. In fact, he wondered if she had any idea at all about offending people or had ever heard the word *tact.*

"The port was over there—not there, anyone can see that from the construction and reconstruction."

He started to make eye contact with Beryl in the rearview mirror. Beryl nodded, sighed, raised her eyebrows, and in the end Archie took a chance and ESP-ed.

"Pain in the preverbal," Beryl ESP-ed back.

When they arrived, Bunnie's light was out, the door was locked, and no sound came from anywhere. Beryl walked around the back, confused and disappointed. Archie knocked on the door and shouted.

Beryl surveyed the garden and soon spotted the burnt remains of an H-Pad carcass under the tree, crashed into the ground. It was embedded upright in the ground, with a small bird with a blacked-out face perched on it. It blinked at her, turned its head to the side, and chirped. Beryl mimicked the bird. It flew off the carcass, and before

H2 had a chance to walk around the corner, Beryl picked it up and slid it into the personal-space pocket in her backpack . . .

"Quick, ma'am, look at this," shouted H2 from the front of the house.

Beryl raced around to see H2 standing by the dustbin, black from an explosion; she lifted the lid and pulled out the mangled plugulator.

"We're as good as toast," said Beryl.

"Pickled as a gherkin," muttered H2.

Archie wondered what food had to do with anything but knew that now was not the time to ask.

Chapter Thirty-Seven

THE OL' FELLA

"Age is only a number to the old—the young never count." —the Ol' fella

Woody showed the address to the waitress.

"Oh, you're looking for the Ol' fella," she said.

"Ol' fella?" said Mex. "No, it's Johnny we are looking for."

The waitress looked at Mex like she was an idiot. "This address is where the Ol' fella lives."

"Ol' fella?" said Pete.

"Aye, the Ol' fella. He stays there when he's creating; other times, well . . . not sure where he goes."

"Everyone knows the Ol' fella," said the boy with a tentative pat on Pete's behind.

"Well, I don't," muttered Mex. She stared at the waitress's powdered face.

"He comes here for his tablet," said the cook, poking his head around the corner. "He says my tablets is the best ever."

Tablet? What the gherkin is tablet? thought Mex. She looked at Woody.

"It's a sweet," said Woody. "Scottish."

Mex looked at him.

"You suck it," said the boy.

"I see," said Mex, still confused.

"I heard he had a tea shop in Glasgow and sold it to some Jimmie guy and moved here to write," said the cook.

"He's a writer?" said one of the customers. "Fancy that. I thought he was an alcoholic."

"No, he writes. Folk come looking for him—when he's here."

Pete turned to Woody. "Maybe there's someone who stays with him? Johnny?"

"Never heard of no Johnny," said the waitress.

"Legless?" said Mex.

"What kind of name is that—Legless?"

The customer looked up from his roll and sausage. "Maybe *he*'s an alcoholic?"

Pete, Mex, and Woody stood outside the café with the directions to what sounded like an old shack in the middle of nowhere, owned by an old writer—of what, no one knew—who could be an alcoholic.

"Finding Beryl, let alone getting home, seems as possible as Woody doing the high jump," said Mex.

Woody, ignoring the high jump comment, waved to the small boy now pulling faces through the café window. The boy waved back and then ran out, clutching a bag of tablet. "Cook says you're to take this to him. He's running out . . ."

The footman waited until all was quiet in the shed, then pressed his ear as instructed by Hilda to the vent with a glass. Hearing nothing, he entered, switched on the remote, and connected it to Hilda's H-Pad.

"What are you up to?" said DBO, switching on her makeshift flashlight.

The footman looked about; the shed looked quite homely. DBO

had spread a few rugs about the place, and in the dark with silk around her shoulders and her hair down—looked friendly, not intimidating at all.

"Would ma'am like a foot massage?" he said.

*D*on and his passengers headed toward Benmore Garden and drove over the bridge, "bearing left" as the waitress had told them.

At first, they argued. Bunnie maintained they had better things to do than deliver sweets to some unknown geriatric stuck out in the back of beyond. "I mean what are we, postmen?" she snapped.

Woody tried to defend himself. "Why not see a little countryside?" he said. "Where's the harm?"

Bunnie, in a huff, stared out of the window as Pete began to mutter about his sensors tingling.

Mex, however, didn't hear a thing she was staring at the road ahead; it was muddy and interesting. At first there were a few new houses and the odd white cottage, but as the road got muddier, the homes became less frequent until it was just fields with cows and sheep. Mex had heard of such things—animals on a field waiting to be eaten—but in the flesh it was more surreal, like the animals were in on the whole thing too.

They parked at the postbox and walked down the dirt track—all apart from Bunnie, who remained in the car with an "I'll wait here," arms-crossed stance, muttering "an entourage to deliver tablet—what next?"

On the fence were two mugs with a half-eaten roll, suggesting that there was more than one . . . or perhaps, as Woody put it, the Ol' fella was not into washing up.

They stood at the front of a stone cottage. The beat-up porch had two seats, one warmed by a mangy old cat that even Mex didn't want to touch.

Don knocked on the door; no one answered.

"There's no one in so let's go," yelled Bunnie from the car.

Don pushed the door open and shouted; no one answered.

Mex, impatient, walked around the back with Woody, shouting, "Anybody in?" They saw a rosebush, some hens around the rosebush, and a shed small in comparison to the Operators' shed. The door was open and a lot of grunting was coming from inside.

Mex stared at the garden. She had never seen anything like it before—broken bits of cars with brambles crawling over them and a couple of hens pecking about. One made a beeline for Mex. She bent down to pat it and it pecked her fingers.

"Get out of it, will yer, that's the dinner," shouted the voice from the shed, followed by a dog barking and the crashing of a bowl. "Look at the mess, you made yer buggar, and who's gonna clean that up? Me, I suppose—yer old fart."

The Ol' fella walked outside. He spied Mex and Woody but said nothing and kept on walking, looking about for something. He scratched his hip as he rummaged around by the side of the shed. "Where's that spade? Put it somewhere." He looked up at Mex. "Cannae find my spade, you seen it? The dog's messed things up in the shed."

Woody pulled it from the veg patch and offered to help.

The Ol' fella smiled, revealing a perfect set of teeth. "Thanks, son."

There was a crash at the front as the cat made a jump at Don, and the Ol' fella ran around like a man of twenty. "What the hell are you doing here? I told you, I'm not interested in your *new build* so you can just piss off." He paused. "You're not from the council, are you?"

"No," said Don.

The Ol' fella's lounge was warm, dark, and claustrophobic. The walls were covered in paintings and photographs of women and shelves of books such as *Legends of the Not So Great* and *The Chronicles of This and That*. The floor was covered in worn mats and the furniture was old and smelly—the whole feel was very Middle Earth, apart from *Woman's Hour* playing in the background.

DJ caught sight of a photograph of a blonde. She was familiar. He tried to recall where he had seen her before as the Ol' fella started to talk with a familiarity that was unnerving.

He told them to take a seat as he made tea in the other room. "But don't make yourself at home," he said, "I've had my fair share of visitors for today."

The foursome looked at each other. Woody mouthed *Is Bunnie okay?* to Don, who, with an *I'll go out and look* shrug, left, just as the Ol' fella brought through a tray with black sticky tea, biscuits, and some tablet. He offered his tray to Mex with a prolonged look and gestured to the tablet. "It's Scottish, very special—from Sheila's Diner."

She picked up a small piece of tablet and a mug.

"You're not from here, are you?" he said.

"Close by," she said with the tablet on her lips.

"And those clothes—you look uncomfortable. I take it they're not yours?"

Mex, wondering what had happened to the old man fumbling about in the shed and why the sudden interest in her clothes, bit into the tablet. The powdery sweet crumbled as the taste of sugar and condensed milk exploded in her mouth. She closed her eyes; nothing could describe the beauty of such a taste . . .

"Oh, my pickled egg," she muttered.

Pete took a biscuit; he wanted a clear head. His intuition was making him feel uncomfortable.

The Ol' fella put the tray on the table, allowing the others to help themselves while he focused on Mex, and offered to read her palm.

"Ma'am, it is an ancient practice of reading between the lines," said Pete. "Perhaps best left for another time?"

Mex had no idea what he or Pete was talking about and didn't really care. She took another piece of tablet and this time washed it down with the sweet tea. It was better than wielding a whip at high speed, better than caffeine after a hard day of whip-wielding, and almost as good as a foot rub.

She went for another piece.

The Ol' fella held her hand and closed his eyes. He was quiet at first and then began to hum chanting noises. *Ooooooom.*

DJ continued to stare at the photo. He was still trying to work out where he had seen the blonde . . .

"She," said the Ol' fella, flicking his eyes open, "is Johnny dressed as a woman. Nothing to worry about; he sometimes likes to tell stories from a woman's point of view."

DJ looked at the Ol' fella. He winked, then ESP-ed, *"And if Bunnie was here, she would have said... 'that explains a lot'."*

Chapter Thirty-Eight

THE LEAD

"You can lead a dog to water but you can't stop him jumping in."
—the Ol' fella

Don took one look at Bunnie sitting in a huff and decided to "leave her to it." A hen pecked at his feet; he bent to pat it and it ran into the shed. Don decided to follow. He slipped inside and, having been pecked several times, gave up on the idea of patting and began to shoo instead—not an easy feat for Don. His only experience of a chicken was it stuffed, sliced, and covered in gravy. He had no idea they could move so quickly, let alone make such a mess on the floor. He continued to shoo until the hen disappeared under a pile of papers.

Don looked around at the mess. He skidded on a newspaper, grabbed a shelf to steady himself, and knocked a notebook to the floor. Scraping off a chicken dropping, he opened the book. On the front was a sketch of Johnny on a motorbike with a blond ponytail and his kilt flowing in the breeze. Don began to read . . .

He roamed the glens of Scotland, telling stories like no other. He told stories for free drink, a free bed, and anything else on offer.
Don turned a few pages . . .
An offer is an offer—never turn one down without serious contemplation.

Don started to flick through the pages . . .

However, if what is on offer has already been offered before and left you wanting . . .

Don began to feel bored . . .

The Ol' fella started to talk of Mex's great adventure, of the years she spent slogging away after men building a reputation. "Now you want to retire in that villa with a balcony by a sea you've never seen," he said, "but she has other plans." He waffled on about robots and Androids, the masses and leather.

The Ol' fella tried to catch her eye; he wanted to ESP her a private message, but Mex was too busy sucking her tablet. It had stuck to her teeth, and it took all her attention.

Mex started to giggle. Her mouth was full of delicious, sweet sensations. *Why do they not have stuff like this on my planet?* She went for another piece of tablet.

"Ma'am, I think perhaps we should find Beryl," said Pete.

The Ol' fella turned to Pete, his eyes crinkling into a smile. "We both know you have no palm for me to read."

"Ma'am?" said Pete. "We should go."

Mex started to breathe deeply—lulled into a slumber of bliss.

Pete turned to Woody: "One more tablet and she'll be down for the count."

"No lifeline, no Mount of Venus; your palm is like a tablecloth," said the Ol' fella to Pete.

Pete looked away. "There's no need to be so mean."

"We just need to know about Johnny," Woody ESP-ed.

"Johnny's a storyteller," the Ol' fella said. "He tells them like no other, sometimes too much, and he can get a bit boring. See all these books?" He gestured behind him. "All about women. I keep telling him women have the depth of the universe. But does he listen? Not him, just keeps writing . . ." He pulled out a book and began to read:

"'Never warm your feet on a woman—they take it personally' . . .

'Socks are death in the bedroom' . . . 'A woman's idea of coordinating has nothing to do with balance.'"

The Ol' fella shut the book and looked up with an expectant face. He saw their looks of boredom and sighed. "Who wants to read that?"

"A bit of humor wouldn't go amiss," said DJ.

"At least he's not mean," muttered Pete.

*B*unnie watched Don as he entered the shed and then went back to her staring. She waited for someone to notice she wasn't there, she waited for Don to come back, and she finally came to the conclusion that no one was coming back because no one gave a damn about her. *Well, we'll see about that,* she thought. *Here I am helping when I don't even need to and no one gives a fig* . . . She stomped to the shed to give Don "what for" and pushed opened the door, a hen fluttered from the top of the door and landed on her shoulder.

She let out an ear-piercing scream. Don started, and the cat which up to now had been in a deep trance-like sleep jumped, snarled, then looked about . . .

"That'll be Nellie," laughed the Ol' fella, "the oldest hen I have ever had—she loves to spook folk."

Nellie pecked Bunnie's cheek.

She screamed again, this time with wild flapping movements that sent Nellie into a frenzy of flapping, along with several other hens which had been quietly snoozing in corners.

"Aye, that's Nellie, all right."

The cat raced to the shed.

The shed was now full of hens flapping and Don, who now considered himself an expert shoo-er of chickens, regained his composure and began to shoo with dignity.

Bunnie asked him what the hell he was doing.

"It's called shooing," said Don with a glare. "It's what farmers do."

The cat began to stalk Bunnie.

"How would you know?" she said, swiping a hen from her feet.

"Saw it on TV."

Bunnie pushed a hen from her feet and skidded on the same bit of newspaper that Don had.

"Mind!" yelled Don.

Bunnie staggered back, backing the cat into the corner, which sent the hens into another frenzy of flying.

"See what happens when you don't"—*crash*—"listen to me," snapped Bunnie. She toppled to the ground, missing a screeching cat by inches. The cat jumped from cans of paint to one shelf and then another, sending debris flying. He landed on the third shelf, skidded on a pile of leaflets, and rolled off the edge. A paw grabbed the edge, and for a moment the cat dangled like spaghetti from a fork as leaflets cascaded to the floor.

As the last leaflet fluttered past Bunnie, she caught a glimpse of some of the words on the cover: *Edinburgh*, *Johnny*, and *free*.

"Johnny," she shouted as the last leaflet fluttered on to a pile of hen poo followed by the cat.

Archie, Woody, Pete, and DJ stood at the door.

DJ picked up a leaflet; on the front, written in comic text, was "*Johnny Gets Legless at the Weekend.*" Underneath was a cartoon picture of a blond-ponytailed man in a kilt hanging over a motorbike looking more than hung over.

"Looks like Johnny's doing his storytelling at the festival," said Woody.

"We've just been there," muttered Pete.

"And it's free," said Woody.

"I could have told you that," said the Ol' fella. "All's you had to do was ask."

HILDA'S EPILOGUE

A worm never turns, it only rolls

Hilda, sipping her chilled sparkly was lying in her onesie watching the only H-Pad working on her planet. Hilda had, thanks to the footman, connected to the remote control sitting on the shelf in the shed. She now had access to all of DBO's operations—and no one had a clue, which was probably not a great thing. Now she knew what women thought of her and, to be honest, she was a little shocked. She had always prided herself in her taste in clothes and her ability to be fair.

Hilda watched Mex bliss out on tablet, she watched Don and Bunnie search the shed, and laughed until her sides split.

She watched as they left for the festival and continued to watch as the Ol' fella talked to the dog. "Look after the cat will yer, I'll be off for a while." She watched as he pulled out a kilt and slipped it on, took off his wig, and brushed his hair into a ponytail. She watched as he pulled out a motorbike, slipped on a backpack, and headed down the track . . .

Hilda looked in the mirror and stared at her kookaburra like hair, she brushed it down and it spiked up again. *Soon that spark plug will be mine and then we'll see who's fair on this pickled egg of a planet.*

****

Would you like to read more? Does Hilda get her hands on the spark plug? Who is the Ole fella? And will Mex ever make it back to Planet Hy Man in one piece?
Book 2 ***Rebel Without a Bra*** is out now at your favourite store...
If you want a taster just turn the page.

REBEL WITHOUT A BRA

Chapter One-The Second Massage

"The rubbing of a toe is greatly undervalued."—An elderly footman

Hilda stared out of the window. It was dark, with no outlook but the wall of the building beside it—hardly a penthouse view.

It wasn't her choice; it wasn't anyone's choice. Even an Operator's grannie would have turned down Hilda's so-called penthouse suite. Beryl claimed it was "temporary."

That will soon change, thought Hilda. *But first things first: overthrow, divide and conquer, overthrow some more, and*—she smiled—*the trappings will soon follow.*

Hilda had watched Beryl's landing on the streets of Dunoon. She also watched as Beryl and H2 left the Argyll. The H-Pad was able to tap into CCTV and gave Hilda a clear picture of Beryl and H2 taking shelter in a doorway. Hilda found great pleasure in watching them huddle together for warmth.

Only the masses huddled.

Beryl rarely shook hands, let alone touched, and there she was closer than a set of glasses on a nose to an Operator of the lowest order—H2, a woman who was lucky to get a nod from a kitchen porter let alone a shoulder from the leader.

Hilda let out a loud, maniac laugh that jolted her snoring footman awake. Beryl's days of leading were numbered.

"Switched the H-Pad on replay. Back to the first arrival," she shouted, then eyed the footman. "How about a massage?"

She wanted to bask in her brilliance, enjoy her triumph and perhaps . . . relax . . . just a little. Soon she was so relaxed she fell asleep and woke to the H-Pad replaying Beryl's time in Sheila's diner, and her footman doing something painful with her small toe.

The footman was staring at a clear picture of Beryl, H2, and Archie looking dry and warm in Sheila's diner with Archie tucking into a plate of meaty food glistening with fat. The footman mesmerised by the eggs, bacon and extra-large Cumbria sausage; had stopped mid manip-ulation. As he watched a large forkful of sausage enter Archie's mouth he squeezed and forgot to stop he could just about taste the gristle . . .

Hilda's mouth almost watered until she pulled herself together.

"Get me more bubbly," she shouted.

"But . . . your bunions, ma'am, I haven't touched them."

"Bunions? The leader has no bunions." She paused for a minute. "This is an earphone moment."

The footman's face filled with dread. "Ma'am?"

"Yes, I think earphones are called for."

The footman gulped.

Earphones were one of the few things never modernised on Planet Hy Man, and were, according to all footmen, a "bastard" to set up.

He gestured about the empty room. "But who is here to hear . . ."

Hilda glared at him; he stopped mid-"ma'am?"

"These are dark times; no one is to be trusted, not even those dozy footmen out there," she said, gesturing to the corridor. "Who knows if they are really dozing?"

He looked at her. Was she mad? The footmen were so old even if they did hear— *which they couldn't*—they wouldn't know what to do or even care if they did. They had, like their out-of-date hearing aids, given up, packed it all in, and were waiting for the day of "shuffling off." The day a letter arrived at the footman's bunkhouse stating . . .

"Service no longer required, pack your things"—which was a mere backpack or two—"the resting home awaits."

The resting home was a place where, rumor had it, old men could finally stop standing and had a view worth staring at.

Hilda motioned a "what are you waiting for?" wave.

The footman, wiping his hands, went to the "only open when absolutely necessary" drawer and pulled out a bowling-ball bundle of ancient earphones glued together.

Resignedly he began to untangle.

"Hurry up," she snapped.

He fumbled as nerves got the better of him.

She grabbed the ball and began to jiggle, pull, and shake while swearing the standard selection of salad vegetables.

"Beetroot and pickled egg, who was the last to use these?"

"You were, ma'am."

She glared at him.

He tried to help, pulling and tugging, then after some undignified slapping from Herself, a set fell to the floor. The footman bent to pick it up with a groan.

"Hurry up," she snapped. "We may be missing something, some thoughts even."

"Ma'am, it is but a mere rumor that earphones pick up thoughts."

"We'll see about that, bring them here."

"But you don't know where they have been," said the footman pulling a face.

"Just hand them over."

The footman, after a ceremonial flick/wipe of his lace handkerchief, suspended them in front of her with a look of distaste.

Hilda snatched them from him, eased the tiny piece into her ear, and stared at the H-Pad . . . she had a perfect view of Sheila's diner.

The waitress handed Archie a brown bag of something, and thanks to the footman, she had no idea what. She threw him a "now look what you made me miss" look.

"Tablet, ma'am, don't you remember?"

"Ah yes," she smiled. "Mex's downfall."

Hilda stretched out her other foot. "What about the other small toe?"

The footman left Hilda's room, pulling faces at the other footman in the corridor.

"Earphones, now," he tutted.

A few tutted, except for one footman—the footman who had just spent his "sleep" night massaging DBO's feet. Without a word or a gesture, he waited for his shift to end and made for the shed.

He coughed at the door as instructed by DBO and waited for her answer.

Earphones, he thought. *I wonder what her in the shed will think of that?*

***

Book 2 ***Rebel Without a Bra*** is out now at your favourite store....

A NOTE FROM THE AUTHOR

I hope you enjoyed the adventures of Mex and her gang.
I would be tickled pink if you did!
I named Beryl, and Don after *big time* characters of my childhood.
I won't tell you who, but they were larger than life and impossible to
forget.

You can find me and my groovy blogs at
www.kerrienoor.com
Like me at

facebook.com/kerrienoorwriter
x.com/kezzamac
instagram.com/kerrienoor

THANKYOU'S

Editor- the lovely Sarah Kolb-Williams
Book cover designer-Thomas Mc Gee and the wonderful libzyyy @ 99 designs
And...
To all those who worked and cooked in BanDuic, my hubby's family Indian restaurant. I was inspired, fed and given the best seat in the house to write.
And...
And of course my hubby who listened, laughed and fed me wine and more wine while writing this great epic.

OTHER BOOKS BY KERRIE

Kerrie A Noor
Planet Hy Man Series
Book 2: Rebel Without A Bra
Book 3 Rebel Without A Crew

Kerrie Noor
Diva Diaries Series
Novella 1:-A Dame Called Derek
Novella 2:- Panto Boy
Novella 3:- Panto Girl

And
Bellydancing and Beyond series
Book 1 :-Sheryl's Last Stand
Book 2:- The Downfall of a Belly dancer
Book 3:- Four Takeaways and a Funeral
Book 4:- Three Angry Women And A Baby

Regards and Cheers
Kerrie

This is a work of fiction.
Similarities to real people, places, or events are entirely coincidental.
No part of this book may be reproduced in any form or by any electronic or mechanical
means, including information storage and retrieval systems, without written permission
from the author, except for the use of brief quotations in a book review.

Rebel without a Clue

First edition. February 05, 2017.
Copyright © 2016 Kerrie A Noor.
Written by Kerrie A Noor.

❀ Formatted with Vellum

www.ingramcontent.com/pod-product-compliance
Lightning Source LLC
Chambersburg PA
CBHW021135190726
48288CB00008B/2672